FRAGMENTED LIVES

Novel

Imali J. Abala

Cover art courtesy of Anne Lutomia

Edited by Tendai R. Mwanaka

Mwanaka Media and Publishing Pvt Ltd,
Chitungwiza Zimbabwe

*

Creativity, Wisdom and Beauty

Publisher: *Mmap*

Mwanaka Media and Publishing Pvt Ltd

24 Svosve Road, Zengeza 1

Chitungwiza Zimbabwe

mwanaka@yahoo.com

mwanaka13@gmail.com

https://www.mmapublishing.org

www.africanbookscollective.com/publishers/mwanaka-media-and-publishing

https://facebook.com/MwanakaMediaAndPublishing/

Distributed in and outside N. America by African Books Collective

orders@africanbookscollective.com

www.africanbookscollective.com

ISBN: 978-1-77921-327-3

EAN: 9781779213273

DISCLAIMER

All views expressed in this publication are those of the author and do not necessarily reflect the views of *Mmap*.

[1]

I was twenty-one years old when I set foot on American soil. Never having lived in an urban city all my life, I was ill-suited for my uprooting, a truth I came to learn only too soon. My story began in an idyllic village of Kerongo anchored in a remote place right on the equator. Our house was the only beautiful brick dwelling in the village for years surrounded with bougainvillea plants that formed a magnificent hedge. Most people owned semi-permanent homes roofed with corrugated iron sheets or grass-thatched huts and, huddled at the base of the hill, none had the semblance of permanence. I always wondered if any of us would survive an earthquake were it to happen. Chances were we would all perish if there was a massive tremble from the earth's belly, shifting the rocks that dotted our landscape off base and squashing every living soul like a gnat between unforgiving fingers.

Those days of my formative years, nothing newsworthy ever happened in our village. The only news we got came by way of word of mouth from a neighbor, relative, passersby, or Father's blue Sony radio. Tidbits of faraway places floated in the wake of our morning or dead of night— Iran and Iraq conflict. The Palestinian and Israel conflict. Yitzhak Navon. Yasser Arafat. America. Japan. China. India. Local news and of neighboring countries, too, floated our way—about apartheid in South Africa. Mwalimu Julius Nyarere of Tanzania. About General Idi Amin Dada overthrowing Milton Obote of Uganda. The Entebbe Raid. About Mzee Jomo Kenyatta. About Daniel Arap Moi. Aah! So much to process for such a young mind unfamiliar with the perils of the world. I could only imagine some of the places I heard about as the news dripped in my mind and vanished like mist on Maragoli Hills in the wee hours of dawn or night; all about things which had little to no bearing on my life. Sometimes the news was sparse, for we were never allowed to touch the radio lest we break it. Oftentimes, Father left it in plain sight, but it was useless to us for he would take the batteries out to minimize our temptation with his priced gadget. Eventually, we learned never to touch it, with or without batteries. Father, like clockwork, turned it on twice daily, especially when he was home. I always awoke at dawn to the sound of the Voice of Kenya station humming tune of the national anthem:

> *Oh God of all creations,*
> *Bless this our land and nation.*
> *Justice be our shield and defender*
> *May we dwell in unity*
> *Peace and liberty*
> *Plenty be found within our borders*

The anthem was succeeded with both a Christian and an Islamic prayers. Then, the morning news followed. No sooner did it end than Father put in a cassette tape of church choir music. He liked Tanzanian choirs best, but his favorite song was *"Umejivalia Ngozi ya Kondoo,"* of a wolf in a sheep clothing. Having committed the song to memory, I seldom listened to its lyrics. For a very long time, I didn't know these very sounds, which came over the wires and dripped through my ears and into my soul over the years, weren't a part of the morning radio entertainment until much later on in life. I just assumed it was. Its tempo, soft and pacifying, sent me right back to deep slumber only to awaken to Mama's calling. Father also turned on the radio at 9:00 p.m. for the evening news and would turn it off after *Matangazo ya Vifo,* news about the dead.

Not many families in our village owned radios. No. Only one other family did besides us and there was a story to it. There was a neighbor whose son worked in Nairobi City. One year, he came home for Christmas holidays as he routinely did when he caused a stir in the entire village, which to this day, people still talk about. The young man arrived home at night when blackness was almost complete. Only sounds of crickets and frogs hummed the night. No one was outside at that ungodly hour, save for those who were night runners, to take notice of what he brought with him. He made a quick stop into his hut where he left his luggage. He made another stop to his parents' house, ate his super and retired to his hut for a much needed rest after an eight-hour trip from Nairobi. The next morning, his mother awoke to people's loud voices emerging from her son's hut. Aware he had company, she did what any Logooli mother could have done. She slaughtered her only rooster and started preparing lunch for her son's guests. Then, she made a giant pot of tea enough for ten people. When it was ready, she marched to her son's hut and knocked noisily on his door to invite her son's visitors for tea. That was when she saw it—a black shiny box on a table. The box had a black round knob to the right side, a long silver wire that ran from the box upward, and two giant black eyes from which voices came. Loud voices true to life. Poor woman, she swooned at the sight of the contraption. A talking box was too bizarre to bear, something she had neither seen nor imagined. All this was to the rapt gaze of her son who came to her aid in pronto; it was useless.

There was no electricity in our village to give us a slice of modernity. No telling when this slice of modernity would make its grand entrance into our village. KTN, KBC, KTV, or even CNN networks were not part of my reality. Watching a T.V. show or a movie was as remote as snow on the Equator. Like the poor mother, I, too, had never seen any music videos or YouTube clips to clue me on life outside my village of Kerongo. I flourished to Mama nightly tales of the ogres and Brother Rabbit. Other stories were about 'naughty' children afflicted with *zindendeyi*—mumps—and advised to carry firewood to *mteembe*—oak—tree, to ward off the illness all the while singing:

Ndendeyi hera ku mteembe—Mumps end on the oak tree!

Ndendeyi hera ku mteembe—Mumps end on the oak tree!

The afflicted child was expected to strike the bark of the tree with the firewood, heeding the message of the song—mumps end on the tree—and sprint back home, never to look back. She told of a boy who neglected to heed the advice. He died of his illness. I promised myself that if I ever were afflicted with mumps, I would dash to the tree with cheetah speed, smack it with my firewood, mustering all the energy in my body and dash back home, never to look at the monstrous tree.

We had no running water or indoor plumbing. We used a pit latrine and bathed in a makeshift bathroom made out of banana leaves and fibers, where a handful of rocks were placed upon which we stood. Occasionally, on pitch black nights, we bathed in the open, giggling under the dark sky. One night, when a night runner struck us with avocados, Father resolved to build a permanent bathroom. That night though, you should have seen us dash into the house. With our wet soap sodded bodies dripping with water, we ran indoors. We didn't care that we were naked. When an avocado struck one of my sisters, a missile that was as fast as light, and being light on our feet, we evaded further assault as we torpedoed indoor to Mama's laughter. The soap suds on our bodies were enough to make anyone break in mirth. We were not amused. Such mischievous happenstance was so trivial they hardly mattered. I called my home a happy permanent camping ground— twenty-four seven for three hundred and sixty-five days.

There was no permanent road connecting our village to the rest of the country save for a dirt road which dead ended a quarter of a mile away from my parents' gate. There should have been a billboard to all visitors to our village with a giant inscription which read: NO WAY OUT: ADVANCE AT YOUR OWN PERIL. Truly, there was no way out. Even if the Ministry of Transport had undertaken a project of constructing a permanent road through our village, it might have been a costly and an odious undertaking. Facets of our small barren community were dotted with giant boulders which spread far and wide as the eye could see. God must have been mad at our people to have created a natural phenomenon that filled the entire landscape with such majestic boulders, pleasing to the eye, but unfit for agriculture. Sullen fires of the sun above the eastern hemisphere were a reminder of God's handy work everywhere. I soaked daily in this bliss, day in and day out. We all did.

There was one primary school where most children in the village attended. There was no shop for us to purchase our daily bread with the nearest market being three miles away of which we trekked on foot any time we ran out of our food supply. There were three major churches: Anglican, Seventh Day Adventist, and

Orthodox. For a small community like ours, there were too many churches to inspire salvation. Instead, they planted seeds of discord that gave birth to occasionally disagreements, of pitting family against family. Brother against brother. Or sister against sister. But these feuds were not significant enough to warrant discomfort. Besides that, hardly nothing happened in this idyllic village save for when someone died or when a wedding happened. Unfortunately, weddings were far in between. To the south-east of the village, laid Lake Victoria. Its blue waters, above which the sun's brilliant glow flashed its shards of light, gave it the appearance of God's beautiful painting, He, the ultimate artist. Blithe filled I bathed in this wonders of nature daily.

This was my humble home. I finished my sixth form in 1981 from Mugoiri Girls High School, Muranga. The following year, when I was about to join the university, an attempted coup d'état to overthrow Daniel Arap Moi on August 1, 1982 happened. Universities nationwide were closed—with Nairobi University to which I had applied and been admitted to being closed for almost a year and deemed a 'den of dissidents with foreign backing.' I didn't understand this terminology, but one thing was clear: this minor distraction had put my academic endeavors in limbo, as a strange marriage proposal would change it all. It was, therefore, not surprising that when a chance availed itself for me to study abroad, I jumped at the opportunity. I had only two options to consider: to go for studies in India or America. I chose the latter. But not before the village gathered in our St. Peters Anglican Church for a *harambee* to chip in the little they had to their name for my benefit—some gave produce, eggs, hens, roosters, goats, sheep, and money—a shilling, five shillings, a pound, fifty shillings, one hundred shillings—they gave it all. I have yet to give back in full their due returns for their investment. Father even kept a ledger with names of all those who gave their donation, which I found—dust and all—when he became one with our ancestors more than thirty years later.

With my parents' permission, against the objection of some of my relatives, and having received all my travel documents—college admission, I-20, visa, and passport—filled with joy, visions of me soaring up in the sky, propelled in a two-winged metallic bird as it sliced through thick fluffy white clouds from my sunny-baked landscape of Kerongo to the faraway land, became my reality. When time came for me to leave home, my heart leapt with glee, happy to make the exit, aware arresting adventure awaited me, with a future promise of many blissful years ahead, of meeting new people, of visiting new places, and of learning a new culture. Aah! The pleasures of a new life were enormous and overwhelming. Nothing could go wrong.

Today, I live in a rundown apartment in the Midwest. My life is still in limbo, cursing my self-imposed uprooting I hoped would breed my salvation—from the rags of my deprived life and landscape—a life to which, in my mind's eye, I must return time and again. There, I am tranquil again. At home. With family. One-by-one, I see them coming towards me, showering me with smiles that melt my heart away with delight, aware I shall never return because I have not weathered the storm of separation.

2

Mama once told me, "Child, in this world, all you need is an education!" She believed my education was destined to swing the pendulum of life in my favor. Her advice wasn't a cliché. Not the way most people thought of it or loosely perceived it. She meant every word of it with every fiber of her being. Edified by her advice, I leapt into the unknown world neither having dreams nor illusions about it. For I couldn't question her counsel unaware that this journey to the center of earth would turn out to be a jagged mountain too steep to climb.

Blind as a bat, I arrived at Dayton International Airport on Wednesday afternoon, August 31, 1983. I wore a turtle-necked, brown floral crimplene dress which came all the way to my knee. It was a cute straight dress I thought looked good on me. I knew I had to make a good first impression on those I met upon arrival. The dress was heavy for summer, but comfortable on the plane. As I waited to deplane, my heart raced with anxiety as travelers, one-by-one, fatigued by travel, rose to pull their belongings from the overhead bins. I, too, followed suit. I disembarked the plane, timid in every way and uncertain of the unknown which awaited me. I walked behind other passengers like a sheep being led to slaughter. It was a slow march to the terminal where I watched folks reunite with their loved ones. Some were greeted with a bouquet of flowers. Lovers kissed passionately. Such show of public affection was alien to me. Families hugged. Others, whom I assumed were foreigners like me, looked as lost as predestined souls for flounder. Their blank eyes roamed about searching for some sort of clarity. Perhaps something or someone. Others marched on, familiar to their surroundings, like a tidal wave. Then, amid this tide, I saw a spec—two eager souls, a man and woman, waving a placard with my name on it. The man was tall, broad-shouldered, and quite portly. His brows were shaggy giving him a very imposing appearance. He kind of reminded me of a German man who had stayed in our home many years ago. He was wearing a brown and white checkered shirt with khaki slacks. The woman was slightly shorter than me, about 5.6 feet tall and averagely built. Her red hair was short, wavy and well-groomed. She had on a floral summer dress, which made her deep blue eyes—the color of the ocean—soft and kind. Though, I was too petrified to see the warmth in her eyes, the kind of warmth I'd witnessed in those passengers who were already familiar with their relatives. Suddenly, fear of gigantic proportion come crowding me. I stood still watching the two strangers with my name in silence.

After a second or so, I sighed a sigh that came from the depth of my being and absorbing the gravity of the moment. As I took my first step towards the couple, I felt my guts churn. 'What if they don't like me?'

As I drew close to them, I said, "Good afternoon!"

"Good afternoon," the man said.

"My name is Upanga! Upanga Kagai."

"I am Dr. Liggett and this is my wife Jean," he said, extending his hand to shake mine. When he spoke, his voice sounded gruff and nasal.

"It's a pleasure to meet you both," I said.

"Welcome to America," Jean said.

"Thank you," I said.

They led me to baggage claim to claim my luggage. At the conveyor belt, I watched as bag-after-bag, of all shapes and sizes, tumbled down. One-by-one, passengers claimed their rightful belongings. Not me. I waited for mine, eye-wide, but it never came. I was later told it had remained at JFK International airport, my port of entry.

'What a twisted fate,' I thought, realizing I had nothing to my name save for my pocketbook. Inside, my passport and $18, which I had been allowed to bring as student allowance, was concealed. This big allowance, stamped in my passport, was evidence of the government's magnanimity. Father had been denied permission to give me any spending money under the guise that I didn't need it.

Suddenly, depression, a malady that would consume my early college years, overcame me. Disappointed, I felt tears begin to sting the rims of my eyelids, aware I had no clothes in which to change. Worse still, because of the long journey, I must have stunk like a skunk. I couldn't hug even my worst enemy.

I struggled to mask my sadness, but Jean saw through me.

"Don't worry," she said as though she had read my mind. "It will all pan out."

I didn't and couldn't respond because I didn't know what she meant by *pan out*. I looked on, lost, and feeling the depravity of my being.

Dr. Liggett, a humble man in demeanor, understood my quandary and did everything he could to calm my nerves.

"Don't worry Upanga," he said, echoing his wife. "Your luggage will be here before you know it." His kind words, which I could barely understand because of his accent, were wasted on me.

"Don't worry!" he said once more. "Everything is going to be all right."

"Okay," I said, but I didn't mean it. He was wrong. My life was never *all right*. It never came close to being *all right*. It had a lot of challenges. Perhaps too much to chronicle. I rolled with every punch that came my way from that day henceforth.

We filled out some papers . . . No, I didn't, but Dr. Liggett filled out the paperwork and then we walked out of the airport to the parking lot.

The afternoon was almost spent when we set foot outside. The hot summer air came flushing against my exposed skin as I walked into the womb of the universe. I had never experienced that kind of heat before. Too intense than my familiar equatorial heat. It was dry, hot and humid. The sky, a deep steel blue, was pleasing to the eye. To the western hemisphere, the sun left giant strokes of red flashed against the unbroken sea of blue.

We got into Dr. Liggett's Buick Century Coupe. I collapsed into my seat which was as soft as satin. As he drove out of the parking lot, I knew my life would never be the same again. Wide eyed, I watched as the unfamiliar Ohio's flat landscape, unlike the mountainous ridges of home and all else there was in my view, fly by like chaff before the wind.

The journey to college—at least so I thought—was a forty-five-minute drive, but it seemed forever. The Liggetts didn't take me to school that evening. I stayed with them for three days. School was still not in session. Jean took this opportunity to school me on what to expect for whom I was forever indebted.

The evening of my arrival to their home, Jean offered me a cold drink, a glass brim filled with ice in which a few drops of Pepsi floated. I took only a few sips, only to realize it was too cold to pacify my parched throat. No. It was the coldest drink I had ever drunk. It hurt my eyes to swallow. I let it be until most of the ice had melted. Unfortunately, by then, the drink had lost all its flavor. After that she ushered me towards her basement. I thought it was where I would be staying for the night.

She led the way to the landing of the basement. I had never seen a room in the ground before. When she opened the door, the stale smell of the basement and that of old clothes ambushed me. It was such suffocating smell. I couldn't see much, but darkness, a profound darkness, as dark as night. A familiar darkness I had seen all my life on those dark nights in the village when the sky was charcoal etched. Too pitch black to see beyond my nose. I stopped behind her unable to move, afraid of what might happen if I went there. 'What if the floor collapsed above us?' I thought. She fumbled for the switch, while I looked on with curious intensity. The air was cold compared to the first floor. She flipped the lights on. I held my breath. That was when I saw it . . . a sea of clothes. The room was painted white and large. It was larger than my parents' living room and lined wall-to-wall with all sorts of clothes in different sizes, different colors, and different styles. There were dresses. Skirts. Blouses. Sweaters. T-shirts. Shorts. Pants. Jeans. Regular slacks. Anything you can think of, she had it in there. There were winter jackets. Spring jackets. Raincoats. Shoes—sandals. Sneakers. Boots. There were different racks for both men and women. I had never seen so many clothes in one room owned by two people.

She reached out for my hand and grabbed it.

"Come!" she said. It was as though she knew I was scared of setting foot in that basement. "There is nothing there to be afraid of."

I took timid steps as I walked behind her until we got to the last step. I stopped, turned back and counted the steps that led to the upstairs. They were twelve in total. In my mind's eye, I tried to conjure-up what I would do were something to go wrong. Perhaps run back up the stairs like a crazed nymph! I turned again, this time, I looked at everything before me with a new eye and mesmerized intensity.

"Choose anything you want!" she said. Her voice was soft and soothing.

Her unexpected words were music to my ears! In that moment, I temporarily forgot all my problems and missing luggage. Oh boy! My heart leapt with unsurpassed joy.

"Really?" I said, grinning ear-to-ear. I felt like a kid who had just been handed a cookie jar filled with goodies.

"Yes!" she said. "Whatever you need." And she truly meant it.

I looked at her with disbelief. I didn't know such generosity existed. Instead of saying something to her, I looked on. All the while, I was thinking of where to begin, what to take, and what to leave, knowing I needed everything.

Everything looked clean and fabulous. I knew it would be a while before I settled on what I wanted.

"No hurry. Take your time," she advised. "Howler if you need me," she added, getting ready to head back upstairs.

Again, I was overcome with fear of being left alone in the basement. A hole in the ground.

"Oh!" Jean said with a smile as an afterthought. "Don't worry. You are safe."

I smiled at her, but mine was a fearful smile.

I had not moved an inch from the time I walked into that basement. I followed her with my eyes as she walked up the steps and until she was out of my view. She left the door open, which was a good thing. So, I could hear her footsteps as she moved about the kitchen. I assumed she must have been preparing supper because I could hear sounds of banging pots and pans, opening and closing of cabinets and running water.

I turned my attention to the task at hand. Before making my first move, I swept the room with my eyes, taking in all there was to see. I also checked to see if there was a bogyman hiding somewhere. There was none. With that settled, my biggest problem was deciding what to pick. It wasn't a bad problem to have. When I finally made-up my mind, I began with dresses. This was a more logical choice. It was what I knew. I took several of those, but because I didn't know my size, it took a while to figure out what would fit me best. I took some skirts. I took some blouses. Bold colors. I loved bold colors—red, orange, white, pink and black. Every girl needs a black blouse and dress. One can never have enough of those. I took some sweaters in different colors. I tried each and every item I picked for the perfect fit. Some made me look very nice. Others made me look like a toad. I didn't take those. After fifteen or so minutes had passed, Jean came back to see if I had made any progress. And, sure enough, I had.

"Very nice!" she said, seeing what I had chosen. "You have good taste."

I smiled.

"You might want to take some shorts and pants too."

I didn't respond. Instead, I looked at her with puzzled eyes. In my village, girls and women didn't wear pants, let alone shorts. Only boys and men did. So, I hesitated in making that selection.

"The weather is still hot this time of year. Shorts will be good . . . maybe a couple would do."

Still, I didn't move. Sensing my reluctance, she marched to the rack with shorts and picked two, which she thought would fit me— a denim shorts and khaki.

"Here, try these," she said, handing them to me. "If they don't fit, pick something else."

"Okay!"

I took and tried the denim one first. The shorts seemed too short and fancy for me. My flamingo like legs were exposed and a sorry sight to see. I felt naked in Jean's presence. Certainly my mother wouldn't have approved. No one in my village would approved, male or female. They didn't represent the right image. Suddenly, I recalled an incident that happened to one of my sisters in the late sixties when she had gone to town dressed in her mini-skirt. Although mini-skirts were fashionable then, some men tore it right off of her. They claimed if she desired to walk naked, they were doing her a favor. She returned home with her eyes brim with tears. Mother warned us against short dresses or skirts for that matter. I was certain she would have definitely admonished me for wearing shorts.

"It feels tight around the waist," I said.

She nodded her agreement and went back upstairs. I tried the khaki pair and it fit me like a glove; it was size four. So I set it aside. I walked to the rack and picked three more pairs— denim, grey, and black. Because I now knew my size, it was easy to choose what to get. I also added a couple of slacks and a pair of jeans.

By the end of it all, I had enough clothes to last me for a while. It was more than those I had in my luggage—two corduroy skirts-black and brown, a blue velvet skirt, two floral chiffon dresses. One was pink and the other was forest green. A couple of blouses-black and white. I also had a towel, undies and toiletries. I didn't care about those at that moment. I had all I needed. My luggage didn't arrive until after three days.

That evening, Jean treated me to a real American dinner: seared lamb chops, mashed potatoes and gravy, and a salad. I enjoyed the lamb chops and potatoes, but skipped the salad because I found it unpalatable. This was how my life in America began over a warm dinner.

3

It didn't take me long to realize that my new culture terrified me. For it was the first time I was living away from my family. Until then, I didn't know I was different. Everyone in my village was Kenyan. The only time I came close to a European person was when a German man, a pious man in every respect, had come to the Orthodox Church for a visit and stayed with us for a week. He was such a character. He was tall, chubby, and walked with a limp in his right leg. His hair came all the way to his shoulders. His beard, similarly, was long and hang below his thin pink lips all the way to his chest. He kind of looked like the picture framed image of Nebuchadnezzar that hang on our living room wall. Only that he wasn't walking on all his fours. Mother had given him a room in our home for the duration. What was odd about him was that he was not only a chain smoker, but also had come with a humongous bottle of whisky. I didn't know what it was then until many years later. Father, being a priest in the Anglican Church, routinely preached against smoking and alcohol as vices that sent one directly to hades. For a religious man, he was such a chain smoker. He smoked one cigarette after another that our entire house smelt of nothing more, but cigarettes.

Two day after his arrival, I confronted Father about it. "Why do you let that man smoke in our house? Isn't it a sin?"

Well, Father looked at me with a confused facial expression. He took a long time pondering my question.

"Child," he said after a while. "The man has been sent here by God to test my faith. Don't *you* see?"

"Oh!" I gasped. 'He must have had such a special connection to the Almighty,' I thought.

"Don't mind him. Soon he'll be gone," he added. "Don't mind him . . . okay?"

"Yes Father!"

"And don't you dare smoke. You hear me? It is still a sin," he added imposing his inflexible will against me. Father believed this to be law and gospel true. He won on this one. I have never smoked for as long as I have lived and never will.

"Yes Father."

I didn't bother him about it after that. It wouldn't have been prudent.

On my third Sunday in America, one of my professor—Dr. Jones—invited me to his Quaker Meeting. This day forever changed me as the reality of my being different smacked me in the face in a most unforeseen way. I awoke to a fine autumn morning determined to bring religion back to my life. Having grown up in the church all my life, I kind of missed it. Church had been part of my weekly routine for years. I figured learning about a new faith wasn't such a bad idea. The sun had already rose up high against an all azure sky when I walked out of my dorm room and headed to Meeting that morning. Its brilliant glow warmed my heart. To say that the sun mesmerized me, would be misleading, but other wonderful wonders of nature I saw that morning captivated me— trees. Most of the trees on our college campus had turned golden as though rushed to usher in the winter months. Those newly bereft of leaves, exposing naked their boughs, stretched far and wide.

Naturally, I assumed these trees were dead. So, I thought they would have been perfect for firewood back in my village. As I inhaled the fresh morning air, I promised to inspect this wonder after Meeting.

Because I had never been to a Quaker Meeting before, I went there ready to nourish my spirit with God's everlasting joy. No sooner had I gotten there than I saw everyone in a prayerful repose. The room was large and still as night. Everyone was so quiet you could have heard a pin drop. When he saw me at the door, Dr. Jones beckoned me towards him. Squeezing through rows of people, I filled the empty seat next to him. He didn't mutter a word, but lowered his face to the floor. I scanned the room again. Everyone was still similarly postured. I, too, followed suit eager with anticipation for the word of God. I didn't see a priest or anyone of that caliber. So, I sat in wait, hoping the man of God would soon show. No one came. No one spoke. There was absolute silence, as silent as a catacomb. I looked at my watch, careful enough to avoid detection. It was 10:15 a.m. I realized fifteen minutes had elapsed from my time of entry. Soon it was 10:20 . . . 10:30. 10.45. 10.55. Still no one spoke. I could only hear people's heavy breathing broken by someone's occasional cough. An impressive silence followed. After an hour had passed, I heard Dr. Jones say, "Peace be with you!"

Everyone chimed in, "Peace be with you!"

Meeting was over!

'What the Hell!' I thought.

Having been ill prepared for the Quaker's meditative style, I admittedly acknowledge this was the longest hour I had ever spent my entire life. I was still absorbing what I had experienced when a kid, a young girl, who had accompanied her mother to Meeting made a pronouncement that forever changed me.

"Mom!" I heard her shrill voice say. I turned in her direction. Her mother was busy talking to Dr. Jones. The girl had on a beautiful pink ribbon pinned on her long blond hair. She had a white-lace dress well-suited for a baptismal.

"Mom!" the girl said again as she extended her tiny fingers towards her mother, wrapped them around her mother's hand, and pulled.

"In a minute!" the mother said. The girl wouldn't let go of her mother's hand. She kept on tugging and tugging at her. I watched with limited interest.

"Mom!" she said again. By the time the mother ended her conversation with Dr. Jones, she turned her attention to the little girl.

"What is it sweetheart?" she said.

"Look Mom!" she said pointing in my direction. She seemed horrified with my presence in their midst. "She is black. Mom, she is black!"

"I turned in the direction of her pointing to see to whom she referred. I didn't see anyone, but me.

I turned and faced the mother and her child with aghast filled eyes. Dr. Jones, too, who had overheard the child looked at me petrified. He was speechless.

Until that moment, I had never thought of myself as black. I was not a color. I was human. I didn't know this reality. I knew I was Logooli that was what mattered in my immediate past.

"It's okay sweetheart!" the mother said to the child calming her agitated soul. "Let's go." She pulled the girl by the hand and whisked her out of the room. I heard their quickened footsteps as they ran down the hall. I heard the sound of an opening door.

After the door fell back in place, Dr. Jones turned to me and said, "I am sorry Upanga. Some people are very ignorant."

The way he pronounced my name was so wrong. He wasn't the only one. Soon, thereafter, I changed it to Mary.

I didn't respond. I looked at him quietly absorbing my new reality. It wasn't the last time I would experience this kind of thing. When I walked out of Meeting moments later, feeling the autumn blues and spiritually unnourished, I forgot to delight in nature's natural glow of the autumn season.

4

Most people claim college years are the best years in one's life. This, for me, was far from the truth. Mine began with a giant cloud over my head, an unshakeable cloud with an occasional sliver of light too bright to matter or make a difference. Because I was new and unaware of American idiomatic expressions, I was doomed to languish in my ignorance. A day after school opened, I realized my world and that of my peers was millions of miles apart. I couldn't talk to them without putting my 'foot in my mouth.' It just happened coincidentally. Words that once slipped off my lips with ease, be it in the classroom, at the playground, or home, now took on a life of their own, making me second guess my uprooting. Time and time again, unaware, I committed cultural blunders of gigantic proportion. Oftentimes, I realized my gaffes only too late or whenever my roommate broke into contortions of mirth.

My first days of classes were catastrophic. Whenever I walked into a classroom and sat down next to someone, I would be shocked to see them stand up and move to another seat. The first time it happened, I didn't think much of it. But when it happened time and again, I knew something was terribly amiss. I couldn't understand it and I didn't say anything about it. My mere presence elicited the reaction. The same thing happened to me in the cafeteria. I was, therefore, forced to conclude that Americans were very unfriendly folks. No one had warned me about it. And if anyone had warned me, I am certain it wouldn't have mattered. After all, no one wanted to be near me, speak to me, or eat with me. Eventually, I decided whenever I went to my classes, I would take a front seat. This was a strategic move on my part given I had a difficult time understanding my professors. Soon, most of my classmates avoided sitting in front so as to not expose their prejudice against me. Some were compelled, by default, the discomfort of sitting next to me, especially if there was no vacant seat available. I could see their discomfort because of how they fidgeted in their chairs. I didn't care because making friends wasn't part of my college goals. I wanted an education just as Mother had advised me. I wouldn't be damned because of their ignorance.

Determined to prove my worth and to let them know I belonged there, sitting alongside them, I studied hard and for long hours. This type of thing was second nature to me. I recalled how I used to study many years ago for hours on end as I crammed for the Kenya Advanced Certificate Education. Oftentimes, to stay awake through the night, I dipped my feet in cold water or drank Nescafe to drive sleep away. It didn't always work out. When I got too tired, my head, without my consent, would fall onto our table only to awake in the morning and go at it again. I toiled like a horse on a wheel those years, keeping my eyes on the prize. It was with this spirit that my roommate taught me a lesson I'll never forget. I was as green as a gooseberry about American culture at that time. Because I didn't have everything I needed, I occasionally depended on her. I sometimes borrowed stationery from her and she, being kind enough, always obliged.

Whenever I studied ahead, I always took notes on all my readings. One day, after taking copious notes, I realized I had made an error in spelling. Being particular about such matters, I decided I would make the correction. And that was when I put 'my foot in my mouth!' I knew I had to erase the misspelled word no matter what. So I turned, once more, to my benefactor for help with this minor problem.

Calling her by name I said, "Might you by any chance have a rubber I could borrow?"

My roommate, who was getting ready too for her classes, stopped her reading and looked at me with horrorstruck eyes. She didn't say anything at first, but the look on her face was enough signal of my unknown transgression.

"A what?" she said in a tone I least expected, slamming her hand on her desk. The desk rattled.

"See, I have something I would like to erase!" I said with mixed emotions. I put my finger to the word I had misspelled.

"We call that an eraser!" she said with a smirk, gritting her teeth and her lips quivering slightly with mirth. She didn't say anything else for a second. And this was the longest second I could remember experiencing.

"Do you know what we call a rubber here?" she said.

"No!" I mumbled, my eyes, like mica discs, rotating from the page I wanted to erase to my roommate and then back to the page. I waited for clarity.

"It is a condom!" she said with a smirk on her face.

"Oh!" I said.

"Here in America, a rubber is a condom," she added, breaking into uncontrollable contortions of mirth.

I felt stupid as my body broke into a cold sweat as the air around me thickened.

'What a mess!' I thought. How could I have known? No one talked about such matters back home, let alone insinuate a desire to borrow a condom. In my world, the topic of sex was taboo.

Stumped, I didn't move. My roommate seemed to be enjoying my gaffe, but I vowed never to make the same mistake again. This was a promise I could never keep. I made more blunders than I can list here. Nonetheless, this incident became a reminder of how my very being and the measure of my spoken words carried with it the weight of my alien being.

My college wasn't very integrated. The majority of the students were white. There were a few students from Asia, Central America, and the Middle East. There were six African students—two Cameroonians, two Ghanaians, a Kenyan, and a Nigeria. All the African students, with the exception of me, lived off campus. There were a few African Americans too. Most of them were in sports, specifically football. Unfortunately, most didn't want to have anything to do with me. One young woman in particular — Alexa—accused me and my ancestors of having sold her people into slavery. She held me personally responsible for this colossal human tragedy no matter who did it. That *I* was responsible for her broken wings. Her floundering dreams, too, were all my fault. Convinced of my guilt, she couldn't dare to have any kind of friendship with me and my sorry lot. I couldn't understand the association my ancestors had to this most despicable and vile act in our human history. For these reasons and these reasons only, a rift between us grew and remained. Being from East Africa, she was far from the truth. My history teacher, while I was in secondary school, once told us that most slaves to American shores were from the West African region. I had no reason to doubt that truth.

There was also the issue of my accent, which Alexa and others claimed was heavy and hard to understand. Expressions like "Oh!

You speak with such a *heavy* accent" became a common occurrence. These folks were oblivious to the reality that they, too, like me, spoke with an accent. I couldn't wrap my mind around this one for I was and I am soft spoken. The words *"heavy* accent" meant very little to me. Besides, I couldn't understand them because they, too, spoke through their 'noses!' Their words wound together in my mind like a wet sheet. So, I couldn't tell why the rift between us was such a jagged cliff, given we faced similar problems.

Those early days of my college years, the place that horrified me most was the cafeteria. There was no *ugali*—corn mash, *chapati*—flat bread, *sukuma wiki*—kale, or *amahengele*—succotash. I couldn't recognize most of the foods they served. Neither did anyone clue me to what they were. A hodgepodge of sorts— Hamburgers. Pizza. Lasagna. Spaghetti. Yes! Spaghetti had the appearance of worms and the idea of eating it simply repulsed me. Macaroni and cheese. Tater tots. French toast. Waffles. Bagels. Cereals—a wide assortment—Fruit Loops, Lucky Charms, Frosted Flakes, Corns Puffs, Apple Jacks. Omelets. Boiled eggs. Fried foods—fries, cheese sticks, chicken. There were vegetables—string beans. Broccoli. Yes! Broccoli looked like miniature trees and very unpalatable to my taste. Salads. Not my favorite at all. I couldn't bring myself to eat a salad . . . I was no goat. Goats ate raw greens where I came from. Not humans. It took me years to get used to the idea of eating raw vegetables. I couldn't profess my love for it. I now eat it because it's good for me. I was familiar with cooked traditional vegetables—*sukuma, muto, kunde, saaga,* and *mutere*—jute leaves—not raw greens, some of which had no English words. Thus, I struggled to find the right foods to eat my entire tenure at college. I never got the freshmen fifteen. Instead, I lost weight. I wasn't the only foreign student with this problem. Other foreign students did too, but I took this minor setback in stride. All the while I thought, 'With time, all will be well.'

Then one day, in mid-September, Dr. Liggett—our International Students Advisor— organized a special outing for all his new foreign students. There were nine of us, with a majority from Asia. I was the only African. His goal was to treat us to America's finest cuisine. I was so excited I could have jumped over the moon.

There weren't many eateries in this small town. There was Frisch's Big Boy, Wendy's, Skyline Chili, and Long John Silvers. He chose Skyline Chili. What a delight it was for us. A change of scenery was a fantastic distraction from the grind of school. For once, I knew I would be eating a meal with other people, not alone as I daily did. He picked us up near the mailbox in a school van and drove the two miles to Skyline. On arrival, Dr. Liggett ordered the food for us because we didn't know what was good on the menu. When our orders were complete and our food served, we went outside and sat down on an empty table. What a glorious and beautiful afternoon it was. The air was nice. Not too hot and not too cold. Just a perfect day for sitting in the open to enjoy an American delicacy. Dr. Liggett ordered hotdogs for all of us—six inches long—filled with oozing goodness. Sandwiched between layers of chili and cheese was the hotdog topped with a dash of onions. I wasn't rushed to bite into mine hoping others would do it first. Dr. Liggett took a giant bite of his to show us proper etiquette for eating a hotdog. We watched him silently. Some of the other students opened their hotdog, but closed it immediately, and put their hands underneath the table.

After he had swallowed his bite, Dr. Liggett asked one of the girls, "Why aren't you eating your food?"

In a timid voice, the girl said, "They gave us the wrong part of the dog!"

"What?" Dr. Liggett said. "It's not dog meat! It's just a name."

We all had a good laugh about it, but I would be lying if I said I enjoyed that hot dog. To this day, I don't like hotdogs. The name alone was enough to make picky eaters like me shy away from this fine American delicacy. I wondered who coined the name. Dr. Liggett never told us. I learned years later that a hot dog—frankfurter—had an international flavor to it, originating from Frankfurt Germany and brought to America as far back as the nineteen hundreds.

5

Several months into my sophomore year, I made a friend. Her name was Brenda. She was a very beautiful young woman from Zanesville, Ohio. She was tall and thin with a tan complexion, which set her apart from most girls at the college. Her spun-gold hair was forever tied in a ponytail, exposing her exquisite facial features. Her sharp brown eyes always shone with excitement. She was the most agreeable person I know. She was full of life, funny, and adventurous. She always brought a smile to my soul even when I felt like crying. At first, I wondered why she befriended me when most of my peers shunned me as though I was afflicted with leprosy. So I thought it was because she once lived overseas and had some exposure to foreigners, or that her parents were military folks who lived on a Military Base in Guam. It turned out not to be the case. I realized my smartness was the yardstick which reeled me from the cocoon of my social isolation. This intelligence was borne out of my hard work, of studying for hours. When my grades exceeded expectations, my classmates noticed. Brenda, who was enrolled in the same class with me, took notice. Suddenly, my *heavy* accent wasn't as *heavy* anymore. I was smarter than her and performed well on most of our quizzes and exams. So she befriended me and we eventually formed a pact: That I would help her study for the Survey of American Literature—and she would help me with my cultural issues. It was a symbiotic relationship. Be it as it may, she took it upon herself to fully integrate me into American society. And truly, she did and even more. She helped me find my first car, which I later named Diamond, and taught me how to drive. I liked her effort because she was full of spunk.

One day, during my second summer in America, Brenda made me an offer I couldn't resist. She asked me out to the movies. There weren't many movie options I town, but I didn't care. Since I had never been to one, my face shone with excitement at the prospect of the outing.

When I told her, "I have never been to a movie theater before," she was intrigued.

"Really?" she said with a giggle as her eyes lit-up. "You are not kidding me . . . Right?"

"No," I said.

"How is that possible?"

"Seriously! I've never been to a movie before."

I was serious. Village life was just that . . . village life. There was no movie theater. The nearest place one could see such wonders, as I was told, was hours away from home. Only those who were well off were lucky enough for such entertainment.

My family back home wasn't as lucky. Growing up, Mama's voice was the proverbial television we needed every night for our delight. She was the best. My siblings and I passed time every night listening to the sound of her voice as she filled our minds with stories about ogres and rabbits . . . Stories laced with wisdom as old as time and transcending time.

Then, my mind took flight to one such a story, of Mama's favorite tale about Rabbit and his friend, Ogre, as it dripped into my ears and to my soul like honey. Once upon a time, Rabbit and Ogre were friends. They always hunted together and were inseparable like twins. One year, there was famine. Most animals struggled to find food. These friends were no different. They, too, had a difficult time taming game. They were hungry a lot. To save themselves, they agreed to kill and eat their mothers. Being crafty and cunning, Rabbit killed a lizard and smeared his lips with its blood. Briskly, he walked to his friend, Ogre, convincing him that he, too, had killed his mother. Conniving as Rabbit was, Ogre fell for his lie, killing his own mother. Soon, with the passage of time, the ravages of hunger began to take its toll on Ogre. He had no one to prepare his meals. He lost so much weight and became so emaciated. Not Rabbit. He was as plump as sugar plumps.

One day, realizing he had been duped, Ogre followed Brother Rabbit home, but not close. He was careful and far enough to avoid detection. When Rabbit got home, he gently tapped on his door. His mother didn't open; instead, she said, "If you are my son, sing our song." Immediately, Rabbit proceeded to sing-

Mama, Mama sunguusa umugoye ninele niine
Aye ninele niine, kaandi niine![1]

She opened the door. Rabbit got in and closed the door behind him. Seeing that, Ogre swore his revenge on his friend.

The next day, Ogre came to Rabbit's home in his absence. He followed the same steps Rabbit had used the previous night. He knocked on the door. Rabbit's mother said, "If you are my son, sing our song." Ogre, who had committed the words to his memory, began sing-

Mama, Mama sunguusa umugoye ninele niine
Aye ninele niine, kaandi niine!

---

[1] Mother throw down the rope so I can climb in!

The sound of his voice was raspy and, therefore, it betrayed him. She knew right away it wasn't her son. She refused to open the door. Disappointed, Ogre went away, but vowed to return. That evening, he came back and listened to Rabbit's singing. He came again a second and a third time. Before long, he was able to imitate the sound of Rabbit's voice.

One day when Rabbit was out, as he always did, Ogre came again. He knocked on the door the way Rabbit did and sang the song as was instructed by his mother. Convinced it was her son, she opened the door. The second Ogre set foot inside the house, he pounced on Rabbit's mother, killed and devoured her. He left behind her entrails and a river of her blood all the way to the forest. When Rabbit returned home that night, he knew exactly what had happened. From that day henceforth, Ogre and Rabbit become mortal enemies.

"'Remember kids,' Mama would say, "every choice you make has consequences!'"

Mama's voice faded away as fast as it had come to me.

"Seriously," I told Brenda. "I've never been to a movie theater."

"Tell you what," she said. "Tomorrow night, I'm taking you to the movies!"

"Are you serious?" I said with disbelief.

"Yes!"

"Then, count me in," I said, ecstatic at the prospect of finally going to see a movie in a *real* theater. Nothing could have been sweeter. For the rest of that day and night, I thought of nothing more, but going out to the movies. I had no memory for such an experience on which to fall.

The next day was Friday, but because of my eagerness to go to the pictures, the day couldn't come sooner. When the hour dawned, Brenda showed-up at my door around 7:00 p.m. I had already had my dinner and ready to expand my horizons, and expanding I did.

"Mary," she said, using my newly assumed name, "I hope you are ready to go."

She was as perky as she could be. So excited she was it seemed as though it was she who was the one having this experience for the first time.

"I know you will like it!"

"I hope so," I said.

It was about 7:15 p.m. when we finally left my room for her car. It wasn't parked very far from my dorm room. As we walked, my head buzzed with excitement. I was certain we were heading to the only movie theater in town located on Lincoln Street. It was about a mile and half from college. This theater showed the same movie for six months in a row. I didn't care about that, but it wasn't where we were destined to end. When we got into the car, it was as hot as an inferno. Brenda started the engine and lowered all the windows. A cool draft swept in from the outside. It felt good. She released her foot from the breaks and accelerated. The car purred gently as it began to glide on asphalt. She drove at a slow pace out of the school parking lot. She turned right to the main road and increased pace. I could hear the sound of grinding tires as the car rolled with ease on the road. As we drew closer to the theater, she revved the engine and the car zoomed fast past it. Drafting wind swept in through the open windows. The hot wind beat against my face making my eyes water. Her action surprised me. I didn't know of another place to watch a movie, but I wasn't the driver and trusted Brenda.

"The movie theater is back that way," I said, turning to steal a glance at the vanishing building several blocks back.

"Don't worry," she said. "You'll see. The theater I am taking you to is the best, a hundred times better than the one on Lincoln Street," she said in an assuring tone. She was all giggles. "My special treat!" There was a glint of joy in her tone.

Mounting anxiety came over me. 'What could be better than the theater on Lincoln Street,' I thought.

After three and half miles of driving, we got to this area where all I could see was a sea of green, cornfield after cornfield. Tall and massive green spread far and wide that it had the appearance of a painting chiseled into being at the hand of a masterful artist. It hummed as the wind sliced through its leaves swaying back and forth, back and forth. . . There was nothing else. There couldn't have been anything else. Soon I saw it. In that massive stretch of green, stood a giant brown billboard with an advertisement of *the* movie. The lettering on it was bold-red, large, but uneven in length and hard to miss. The billboard was the only artificial landmark in this expanse of pure green and naturalness.

"See Mary," Brenda said excitedly. "That's it . . . That is our movie!"

"In the cornfield?" I said.

"Yes. We are almost there!" she said.

Sure enough we were. After a mile or so, she swerved to the left into this open space where I saw the largest screen I had ever seen. It was as high as the skyscraper and as wide as stretching earth. We were not the only folks there. There were college students and regular folks, too, ready to enjoy a night of splendid wonder. The smell of popcorn dominated the air mixed with a natural earthy fragrance.

Brenda found our spot and parked the car. She killed the engine. We walked out and made for this small white building where we purchased our tickets and popcorn. It was also in this building where the movie was broadcast to the screen. By then, it was already getting dark all around and about us. The only thing separating us from the cornfield was the giant screen and nothing more. Behind us and around us, lay miles and miles of corn. We were so removed from civilization it made me feel uncomfortable.

As we walked back to our parked car, the place was now buzzing with activity. Lovers were busy frolicking. There were those who seemed to delight in their drinks, perhaps beer or liquor. Loud music sounded from every car. Save for approaching cars with full beams, all was dark. Late comers turned their headlights off immediately on arrival, found an empty spot and parked their vehicles. Hurriedly, we raced back to our car with our popcorn and coke in hand. Brenda opened the car and we slid back inside. She pulled a speaker and hung it against the side of her window and turned-up the dial. Soon, music blasted into our car and ears. What a euphoric moment! I closed my eyes to listen.

"The movie will start soon," she said.

I faintly heard her voice above the blustering music from people's speakers and our own. After what seemed like a lifetime, Brenda nudged my left side. I opened my eyes to see. There was pitch blackness now, as dark as a dungeon. They must have turned off all the lights. Up above the sky, I could barely see anything. Only black void of nothingness remained. Not even a solo star.

Not even a firefly. A commercial came on flooding the cornfield with light. What a blinding light. It was an advertisement of an upcoming movie. I don't remember the title now.

Our picture came on. I watched with the curious intensity of a child. At first, a list of the characters' names scrolled up followed by the movie title-

a NIGHTMARE on
ELM STREET

I sat on the edge of my seat as the introductory scene began—of a man working with his tools, sharpening his weaponry—knife. A young woman ran in a dingy hallway to loud ominous music. The sound effects were enough to make my skin crawl with fright. I came close to jumping out of my seat. The scene was very captivating. An image of girls jumping rope flashed. A small hand gently brushed in the dirt. Before I knew it, the same hand appeared in my view, holding a white piece of chalk and drawing intricate patterns on the ground. It reminded me of my formative years. I had played this drawing game time and again, learning my ABCs and committing them to memory. I was captivated. It didn't take long for me to become petrified as my reality fused with the movie's fantasy and horror came flooding my sensibilities. In that cornfield, at that hour, I was so spooked I could barely bear the horror on the screen. I was too scared to see it through. In my naiveté, I knew Freddy Krueger was lurking somewhere in that cornfield ready to come for us. Shred us to pieces. No. Shred me to pieces. I had never experienced such fear in my life, ever.

Brenda didn't resist when I told her to take me back to my dorm. She did, but Freddy's image haunted me for years. Brenda never stopped making fun of me for chickening-out from watching a simple horror movie, my first movie ever. I never forgave her for terrifying me to my wits end. To this day, I hate horror movies and you couldn't pay me to watch one.

6

I should have labelled all my adventures with Brenda as "My Travels with Brenda!" Any experience I shared with her was always my first. Though designed to make me embrace the American culture, oftentimes, some of these experience had the opposite effect. I doubt that was Brenda's intention. It just turned out that way and magnified my disillusionment about American life.

There was hardly any social life in Wilmington. It wasn't like other urban cities in America —Boston, Cleveland, Chicago, Minneapolis, Nashville, New York, San Francisco, Washington DC—vibrant with entertainment and activities. Wilmington was a dead town, dead to students who desired evening entertainment, and dead to those who yearned for a place to release the stress of their heavy college work. There were no nightclubs to go dancing; though, there may have been a bar, but not a nightclub. That was why, one day, Brenda and I took a "clubbing" trip to Cincinnati.

I was just as excited to go on this outing as I had been the evening we went to the movies. Being a preacher's daughter, I had never been to a club, ever. Hours leading to our trip, we made every effort to look our best. I wore the best thing I had; a small black short-sleeved silk dress I had gotten from Jean a year back. I put on a pair of my black pumps, which added an inch to my height and made me look exquisite. Brenda, too, looked stunning in her rose-colored attire. It came slightly above her knees. Her gold hair, for once, was trimmed short and came to her shoulders and not tied in a ponytail. With a pair of short dangling fake-gold earrings, she looked gorgeous. Her shoes were black, but with a slight higher heel than mine and shone brilliantly in a glow light that I could see my own reflection on them. Before leaving for the one and hour journey, we made sure we had enough spending money, put gas in the car, and checked the pressure in the tires. Only then did we set off. This was Brenda's second way of getting me to experience a *true* American nightlife.

We left campus around 6:00 p.m. as dusk was fast approaching and the heat of the day had ebbed to a comfortable warmth. It was a spectacular evening for a girls' night out. Nothing splendid happened along the way until we drew close to Kings Island.

"Mary!" Brenda said. "Our next trip should be to Kings Island."

Before I could answer, she added:

"Have you ever been to an amusement park?"

"No," I said. "What is it?"

"That!" she said, pointing to an approaching location to the left of I-71 where fast-paced machines moved faster than any of the locomotives I have ever seen.

"I see!"

"Then it's settled!" She said affirmatively. "Next week, we have to come to King Island."

"Sure!" I said. "No arguments from me!" I didn't know to what I had just agreed.

Road tranced, Brenda zoomed along the highway. We passed the amusement park as I watched it with curious intensity. Although the evening was already advanced, being summer time, the sun still shone brilliantly against the west blue sky. I saw people strapped in fast-paced machines fly up-and-down. Some screamed to their hearts delight. Even as we neared Cincinnati, the jolly voices of those people I had heard at the park, spun about in the machines like yarn on a spindle, and moved me with memory. I yearned for the experience.

We arrived at Cincinnati a little bit after 7:00 p.m. It turned out neither of us knew the town. I had assumed Brenda did; unfortunately, she didn't. When we got to downtown, we found parking for our car, got out, and did a little bit of asking around for a good place to eat. We figured it would be easy to ask about a nightclub once there. Someone recommended a Chinese restaurant which was a stone's throw from where we parked. While we were eating, though I don't recall what I ordered, Brenda asked our waiter if he knew of a good nightclub. He suggested a club which was only a block away from the restaurant. He claimed it was the best nightclub for young college students. I don't remember if we ever told the guy we were college students. Perhaps, it was our physical appearance which gave us away. To avoid the hassle of looking for parking, we opted to walk to the club. It didn't take us long to get there. As I write now, though, I admittedly don't remember its name.

It was almost 9:00 p.m. when we got to the club. It was in a giant brick building nestled amid other similar structures. Already, the night owls were beginning to make their appearance to there. I was kind of nervous about this outing because I was out of my element! A preacher's daughter ought not to patronize such establishments. When we got to the door, we paid our entrance fee of five dollars. The bouncer, a giant man well suited for his job, named Lou, let us in. Once inside, the dimly lit club was loud and had a split floor. Up above the entrance, there were a few steps that led to the second floor where music blasted as the neon lights flashed. Already, multiple people were busy boogying. On the main floor where we stood, there was a large stage draped with red curtains. There were also wooden chairs and tables arranged symmetrically facing the stage. A regular club goer told us there was a fashion show that night. And if we liked, we could watch the show and later go dancing upstairs. No other details were given about the show as though it were a secret affair.

We thought about it a bit. Brenda suggested we watch the fashion show first, hoping the evening would culminate with us on the dance floor. I agreed, knowing I was no dancer. It was settled. We found our seating close to the front so as to maximize the pleasure. The red curtains on the stage were still drawn, but we didn't care. We watched as droves of people came in, both men and women. Some opted for the dance floor; others joined us expecting an optimum experience.

A few minutes after we were seated, a man whom I assumed to be the owner appeared on stage to announce the show. He didn't seem well dressed for the evening like most of the club patrons. And if he had, he didn't make an impressionable appearance.

"Hey folks," he said. "Thank you all for coming! Our show will be starting momentarily. Enjoy!" And with the tip of his hat, he walked back stage as quickly as he had appeared. So, we sat patiently in wait and eager in anticipation.

Meanwhile, loud music upstairs continued to blast the air. It wasn't like the kind to which I had become accustomed to—Cindy Lauper's "Girls Just Wanna Have Fun," Teddy Pendagrass' "I Just Called to Say I love You," Madonna's "Material Girl" and "Like a Virgin," Jermaine Jackson's "Let's Get Serious!" Or Diana Ross' "Upside Down!" A couple seated next to us lit their cigarettes and started puffing. Smoke wafted our away. I doubt if this was intentional, but it annoyed me to my wits end, for I hated that foul smell of cigarette smoke. There was a fan above them, which blew smoke in our direction. Had we had a choice, we could have moved, but there was nowhere else to sit. Besides, it would have been pointless. Smoking in public was as common as people with their cellphones in modern day America.

A waiter approached us to ask if we wanted anything to drink. Brenda said yes.

I didn't know what they served so I didn't say anything.

"What do you have," Brenda asked. She read a litany of drinks off her list. None sounded familiar. I let Brenda choose first.

I didn't want to drink alcohol because Father had warned me against its perils for years. It was a sin!

Brenda ordered a glass of red wine.

I chose Long Island Ice Tea. The word 'tea' was the reason for my choice. The waiter left and returned momentarily with our drinks. We paid her and then she left.

When I took my first sip of my drink, it didn't taste anything like the tea I was accustomed to drinking. I thought maybe that was how American tea tasted. Kenyan tea was flavored with tea Marsala or ginger spices.

"Do you like it," Brenda asked.

"I'm not sure," I said.

She laughed.

I don't know if she knew what it was. If she did, she never clued me on it, at least not that night.

After several sips, I kind of liked it. It didn't taste as strange as it had at the beginning. When the curtains fell and the stage lights flashed, I couldn't believe my eyes. My jaws nearly fell to the floor. I took another sip of my drink, swallowed, and squinted my eyes as the first model made her appearance on stage.

She was a large broad-shouldered woman. Dressed in a red lacy flamboyant garb, the bulkiness of her physical mass gave her identity away. Around her neck, a flimsy feathery black scarf hang. Her bra must have been size forty-four with a triple D cup, for her bulging boobs popped on her chest like giant melons. What an eyesore! Her brunette hair came slightly above her shoulders. Her lips were pencil-lined brown with a crimson-red lipstick. Her lips were so red it seemed as though they had been dipped in blood. She had no hips to speak of, making her exquisite physique strangely disturbing. Looking at her, it was difficult to tell whether she was male or female. The protruding hairs from the red stockings she wore was evidentiary hints of her identity. She paraded daintily across the stage.

After her, other "women" followed, but it was hard to tell, too, whether some of them were male or female. Or rather, were they androgynous? At times, the hoarseness of their voices when they spoke was a clue; others, it deepened their mystery. Some were beautiful, as beautiful as a youth, having mastered the rudiments of being female—hair, make-up, clothing, bouncing in high heels, or hand gestures. They were no different from any other women I knew or me. Amid it all, I was confused with this kind of thing. If I told my mother about it, she wouldn't believe her ears . . . And so, as I sat there watching the show, I wondered what the Good Samaritan who guided us in this direction might have thought about us.

I looked to Brenda for clarity. She shrugged her shoulders and that spoke volumes.

I turned my attention to the stage once more. Another model was making her appearance. Her black purse was daintily tucked under her left arm. When my eyes fell to her legs, pencil thin and bowlegged, they were such sight. She had on white-stockings through which dark hairs were etched. Her high-heeled shoes were so high they were worse than stilettos. They made her bowed legs more magnified that a soccer ball could have passed through them.

I turned once more to Brenda, but all she could say was, "Just watch the show!"

I did. Woman-after-woman who came on stage, there was something odd or unnatural about her appearance. Common sense told me those weren't real women, but I wasn't there to make that determination. What a façade! Some were betrayed by razor rashes on their chin or mustache covered with heavy makeup. I would soon learn what we had witnessed was a Drag Queen Show . . . That was before Ru Paul became known as the queen of the Drag Queen Shows. What an eye opening scene!

After the fashion show was over, we went to the dance floor, but we didn't last long. We were mistaken for lovers. Protesting we were not brought with it other complications. A few women propositioned us. Feeling uncomfortable about the whole ordeal, we left the club after about a half an hour.

By then, my head was buzzing in a strange way . . . An unfamiliar way. The Long Island Ice Tea had done a number on me. In my foolishness, I had not asked our waiter what went into the drink before I bought it. 'Tea was tea!' I had thought. I realized it only too late that my drink was potent—there was gin, vodka, rum—mixed with lemon, triple sec, and gomme syrup. When we left Cincinnati, I was already under the influence of alcohol. I felt very disappointed with myself for not heeding Father's advice—never to drink alcohol because it was a sin. I knew I would surely end-up in hell. I vowed never to drink alcohol again, but this was a promise I broke many times. We drove back to college in silence never to speak of the experience again until now as I pen it to paper.

A couple of weeks later, we were back on the road again. This time we went to Kings Island as Brenda had promised. I wore my blue jeans and a white t-shirt. Brenda was similarly clad, but with one difference. She had on a pink t-shirt. Before leaving town, we passed through K-mart where we each bought a cap to shield us from the scorching summer sun. Mine was white, while Brenda bought pink; both complemented our t-shirts. Good thing we did that, for the long wait in the sun for rides made it a more rewarding purchase. Though, I thought the few minutes of sheer terror on the rides was not worth the wait and money. I am sure amusement park lovers might beg to differ. There weren't any surprises this time. Brenda explained everything we were to see and do. Soon, I found myself, after an hour of standing in line on a hot sunny day, strapped in a ride called the King Cobra. Before I knew what was happening, this contraption inclined up, and spun us about in a loop, flipped us upside down, and plunged us back down in the most devastating way. I heard the clackety-clack sound of the Cobra as it, snake-like, wound itself about. I screamed my heart out, but I knew no one heard me. We were all screaming like lunatics. When the Cobra came to a screeching halt, I understood why people screamed during the ride. But that wasn't all. What I couldn't bear was the dizzying effect that came flooding my senses. I nearly fell down because of it. Luckily, Brenda was nearby to shield me. This incident was enough to make me vow never to get into any of one of those contraptions ever. This was a promise I have surely kept to this day; it was a once in a lifetime experience and I was glad to have done it.

7

When I joined college fall of 1983, I had never held a job in my life, had no personal income, and depended on Father for all my personal needs. Before I left home, Father had paid my tuition in full for my freshman year. Unfortunately, and as luck would have it, a month before I began my sophomore year, I received a letter from one of my brothers telling me Father had taken ill. It was a serious illness for which he had been admitted to hospital. There was no telling when he would return to good health. This news hit me hard, for I knew I was in serious trouble. No one else could help me now. Not even my mother who had never held a job outside the home. Not even any of my siblings. The American dollar was too strong for their meagre earnings to put a dent to the financial support I needed. Given this truth, I was certain there would be no further monetary assistance from Father or home. What a complication! It was one I had not anticipated. So, I had no choice, but find ways to fend for myself and find it fast.

If Father's illness were not enough, I had another minor problem. On my landing at the port of entry, my passport had been rubberstamped and dated with a warning that read:

BEARER NOT PERMITTED TO WORK

The writing was in bold red capital letters which couldn't be missed. It terrified me. How could I now survive without Father's help or if I wasn't allowed to work? It was humanly impossible. Surely, something had to give way; otherwise, my very being and survival was in serious jeopardy. This minor complication compelled me to seek other alternatives. I had no choice. None whatsoever. My roommate told me to try my luck with college facilities. There were some employment opportunities. It wasn't difficult to find work on campus, especially since the job that landed in my lap was janitorial, specifically cleaning students' dorms. This was one of the toughest jobs I ever held. It tested my being and patience and taught me a little bit about human nature. One of the chilling aspects of it was seeing the looks of fellow classmates as they ran into me in their bathrooms. Oftentimes, they looked at me with disdain. This look extended to the classroom, making them avoid me even more. I had to remind myself, through it all, that I wasn't in college to make friends, but to get an education. The worst part, too, was what some of them did, knowing I would be the one cleaning after them. They would poop in a bucket and splash their fecal matter in the hallway for me to clean. This happened a lot on weekends and in one particular dorm, The Penthouse; its occupants were mainly male. Some resorted to this tomfoolery after guzzling beer excessively, even if it was not allowed. This didn't last long, because after complaining to the R.A. and the Director of Residence Life, the misbehavior was squashed. The women's dorms were slightly better. I thought some understood my plight even though I never told them. They tended to keep their areas clean. After several months into the job, I asked for a change in assignment. I couldn't handle it, for it was emotionally draining. And that was the best thing I could have done for myself. I was reassigned to the LVC center where my responsibilities included taking audio visual equipment to classrooms and setting the projectors for professors. This took some learning, having not operated any type of machines. This move turned out to be a blessing in disguise. I would take my work with me and used the opportunity to study while I waited for the class period to end. I wasn't allowed to leave the equipment unattended. This added study time and improved my grades tremendously. Later, I would also add duties of a librarian to my sleeve. My good grades were an inevitable outcome of this and helped garner scholarships from the school for being smart. Having learned the secret to get scholarships, I was relentless in its pursuit. It worked like a charm.

Between my part-time job and school, I hardly made enough money to make ends meet. No matter how many hours I put in— sometimes more than forty a week—it was never enough to meet my living expenses or school fees, not until I started getting academic scholarships. This forced me to seek Dr. Liggett's help. I knew if anyone could help me, he was the one. When I went to see him at his office, he suggested I apply for a work permit from the office of Immigration and Naturalization Service. So, I asked him if he could help me. He agreed and went to the greater extent of not only helping me with the paperwork, but also took me to the INS office in Cincinnati. I applied for the permit and got it. As long as I had mitigating circumstances warranting the request, those days, it wasn't hard to be granted a permit. Mine were dire.

Soon thereafter, I sought work outside college. It wasn't easy at first, for I needed a job that paid slightly more than minimum wage. It took me a little bit over two weeks to land a night job at Airborne Express. My shift was at eleven to five in the morning; consequently, there would be no sleep for me. For a while, this was a sacrifice I was willing to make. My responsibilities included sorting mail and packages on an assigned conveyer belt. The packages snaked along it and I had to inspect them for appropriate zip codes, removing those that didn't belong. Sometimes some of the packages looked small, but were as heavy as rocks. Oftentimes, when there was a jam, I fought with each item that flew my way to minimize a pile-up. It almost never worked as I lost the battle to the speed of the belt. The items were then loaded either on planes or delivery vans. This was a taxing endeavor. The job demanded sharp eyes and speed. I was still young and sharp, and I didn't falter in my duties. I was paid $15 an hour, four times more than the minimum wage of $3.25. I was happy to forego a few hours of sleep for the pay.

The only snafu I had was transportation. Because I had no car to go to-and-fro to work, it became a problem I had to fix and fix fast. At first, one of my friends who worked at Airborne Express offered to give me a ride whenever I needed it. He was a good fellow who demanded nothing from me. Not even gas money. Unfortunately, even good things have their limits. It didn't take long for me to realize our arrangement was too much of a hassle for him than was warranted. It was an unsustainable deal. He, too, was a student and, sometimes, school and his other personal needs got in the way. Again, I had to put on my thinking cap and thinking I did. Nothing of substance came to mind out of this contemplation save for finding other folks willing enough to step in when my friend wasn't available. Without money, I had no solution.

While I was still considering what to do, Divine Providence interceded in my favor. My father, amid dealing with his illness and other family responsibilities, sent me $1000 towards my tuition. I was so excited I could have jumped over the moon. The money, though meagre, didn't come close to a fraction of my tuition. Neither was it enough to offset my other needs!

'What to do! What to do!' I thought. For once in my life, I was forced to make an impactful decision without anyone's advice. Before then, my parents made all the decisions for me. It was their responsibility. Their choices were law and always made for my benefit. Not this time! I was on my own. In foreign land. This decision was mine and mine alone: to either purchase a car or pay tuition. I chose the former! This was a risk I was willing to take. And if I faltered in judgement, I would take full responsibility for my action. I needed transport to work. With a job, I was certain I could support myself, aware money from home wasn't as reliable as an old wheel-horse or sustaining. Naturally, I turned to Brenda for help and she was more than willing to render her services. Thank goodness for her kindness.

This goes without saying that I had never driven a car in my life. This turned out to be another complication I had to face. Back home, only *rich* men owned cars. Not even families from the *middle* class. No, the middle class didn't exist. We had the rich and the poor. Young folks, unless they were born into affluence, only coveted the prized machine. Even something as basic as a bicycle was out of their reach. I was one of those unlucky mass. Now, for my survival, I needed a car to get a license . . . It was my fundamental reality and key out of all my trouble . . . If that were to be case.

Like everything else in Wilmington town, there was only one car dealership. Therefore, one sunny afternoon, Brenda and I drove there to look around for a car. I had no intention of buying one that day. Given my limited financial standing, I couldn't spend more than what I already had. Being a Saturday, the dealership was crowded with folks looking for vehicles like me. None of the salesmen came after us. Perhaps they thought we couldn't have been serious in our quest. Someone once told me college kids were notorious for loitering at dealerships for the latest rides without an intention to purchase. This was a good thing because we were able to walk around without the pressure of a salesman. We walked tirelessly amid a sea of fantastic looking cars—Buick, Cadillac, Ford, Chevrolet, Toyota, Honda—anything one could think and dream of, they had it. Soon, sadness came crowding me. 'If only I had money!' I thought, 'I would have bought a brand new car!' They had plenty of those, but this was only wishful thinking. I couldn't get anything beyond my means. I had to ground myself in reality. After looking around for almost a half hour, my eyes landed on *her*: a white hatchback Honda Civic. I fell in love with *her*. She was the right size and the sticker-prize, a whopping $850, was within my price range. She was small and clean. There was no rust on her exterior; this was the only thing I looked at and could judge. Nothing more!

"I want this one!" I told Brenda with excitement. My resolve reminded me of something a friend had once told me about house hunting. If you find what you are looking for, you'll know . . . I *knew* I wanted this Honda.

"Really? Are you sure?" she asked.

"Yes! It has my name on it."

"I don't see it," she said jokingly.

"I am serious. I like it!"

"Well then, if you say so, who am I to disagree?"

"Then it's settled!"

"Yes, if you say so!"

We walked inside the dealership office to make an inquiry about the car. I let Brenda do all the talking afraid my *heavy* accent might come in the way of a good deal.

The salesman was a good fella. His eyes were sharp and shifty. He asked us to take him to the car we had identified as we walked back outside.

"Sure!" I said, leading the way. It was only two rows from the office.

"This one!" Brenda said after we had returned to the lot.

"Nice car!" the fella said. "It's a 1980 Honda. It came in yesterday!"

"Does it run?"

"Does it ever!" the fella said. "It runs as smooth as the Devil's mill! . . . If you would like, you can take her for a spin!"

The fella's remarks erased any doubts I might have had about the car. And truly speaking, I had none. I trusted the man as much as I trusted Brenda. Besides, I didn't think white folks could be dishonest. I thought if there was anything wrong with the car, he wouldn't have let us test-drive it. I was sold, never thinking anything of it.

"Sure!" Brenda said exuberantly.

The fella went back to the office and returned with a key. Brenda handed him her license for inspection, signed some paper and within no time, we hopped inside.

As Brenda started the car and revved the engine, my mind was already buzzing with excitement at the prospect of *owning* it. Me, Mary Upanga, I was about to be a car owner. Who knew! The thought had a good feel to it. The car would be mine and mine alone . . . No one else, but me. It added some air of importance to me, not that it mattered to anyone else. I imagined driving back home to our village to rapt gazes of villagers. I imagined them waving at me with exuberance. Their smiles of glee would be a signal of my material success. Uniformed in their green tunics and mesmerized by the slick-shine of my metallic wonder, I imagined the primary school pupils watching me from their wide open classroom windows. For me, too, in my younger years, was like one of those eager souls, watching and wishing to my heart's delight to own such a wonder whenever it traversed our space. I never knew I would, someday come close to owning one. Not to mention . . . that I would be the first, among my siblings, like Father had been the first man to own a car in our village. It was a white Renault. It died on him on his way from Kisumu, a nearby town, to home. No one knows what became of it. I would have to exercise care in breaking the news of my purchase to Father. He might be heartbroken to learn I had spent my school fees on buying a car. That revelation would have to wait. For now, I needed transportation to earn a living and that was all that mattered.

As we drove along, I had no idea what to look or listen for, never having any familiarity with automobiles. We drove around town for a while. When we returned to the dealership office moments later, I purchased the car and later named her Diamond, for she was truly my diamond and priceless. The next day, Brenda started teaching me how to drive. That was before I even got a learner's permit. Thank goodness for living in a rural area. By the time I got the learners permit, I had already become a pro. Sometimes, I would drive alone to work, praying I would get there safe and sound. I knew what I was doing was wrong, but necessity sometimes defied rational thought . . . mine was to be as careful as I could, observing all the laws of the land even if I was breaking one. And as Jean once told me, it all *panned* out. I got my license after three months. Feeling free as a jay bird, I began to take on more hours of work to recoup the money I had used to buy the car.

My first three months with Diamond were sweet and smooth sailing. I got in more hours at work, which meant more money came my way. What was a liberating feeling! For once since my arrival on American soil, I could buy some of the things I *wanted* without feeling guilty that I was compromising something. These were not my needs. My needs were great, but my wants were meager, far in between. Then one night, chilly as hell, as I was about to go to work, I started Diamond. She didn't purr after I revved her engine the way she always did; instead, she coughed like an old man suffering from tuberculosis and went silent. No matter what I tried, I couldn't elicit a murmur out of her. Before long, not knowing what I was doing, I flooded her engine. Eventually, I gave-up on her and going to work altogether that night.

I returned to my room, dropped my purse on my bed, and frantically started looking for change to call off work. It wasn't hard to find change for a dollar from one of my peers. Hurriedly, I made my way to a payphone. Luckily for me, on that night, the phone wasn't occupied. I placed my call and returned to my room deflated.

The next morning, Brenda and I towed Diamond to a mechanic. Having tested the freedom of a car, the thought of not having one was dizzying. At the shop, the mechanic opened the hood and inspected the engine.

"Wow!" he said after a while. "How long have you had this car?"

"Almost four months," I said.

"Aah huh! Did you have any problems with it?"

"Not until last night."

He peeped inside again and took out some goop, which he inspected.

Shaking his head, he said: "They sold you a lemon!"

You can imagine my confusion. "What *lemon*? I hadn't bought any lemons!"

The guy laughed!

"Not those lemons, silly!" Brenda said.

"Oh!" I said. "What do you mean?"

"This car! . . . Those sons of bitches sold you a lemon."

"How is that?" I said.

"He reached inside again and scooped something. I didn't know what it was.

"You see this?"

I looked.

"This gook is sawdust! Someone messed with your transmission, which messed with your engine."

"Oh! Boy," I said.

"Your engine is tossed! Out of commission!"

'What to do then?' I thought. I had no money saved. The little I had earned I had already applied to my tuition and I needed a running car.

"Tell you what!" the guy said. "Give me three days. I'll go to a junkyard to see if I can find a used part for you."

"Okay!" Brenda said. "How much will it cost?"

"I won't know until I come back."

"Okay!" I said.

"Then it's settled," he said. "Three days."

Meanwhile, Brenda let me use her car, to-and-from work.

Sure enough, after three days, which was Friday and my payday, Brenda and I returned to the mechanic's shop. He had found another engine for Diamond and fixed her. It cost me another $350. After that my little Diamond was truly a diamond among many. She never gave me any trouble again. I drove her for six more years without much of a hitch. Not until I had moved to Columbus, Ohio years later. That was when I drove in a stagnant water after a deluge and killed her.

Well! May be, I didn't quite kill her, I came close. I knew a friend who knew a friend who claimed he had the cure for used cars like mine . . . even though Diamond was more than a car to me. She and I had been close friends for a very long time. I agreed to give her another second chance at life. My friend told me about a Kenyan mechanic who owned a garage and had offered to revive her for me. I towed her to his garage. He took her apart, piece-by-piece. I wasn't there to see it, but when I went, hoping to be reunited with Diamond, I was dismayed to find her in pieces, dead, and never to be whole again. She was useless to me at that point. I had a hard time parting with her; she was and had been my prized possession. That day, I said goodbye to my Diamond with a heavy heart.

Soon thereafter, the same friend who had recommended the mechanic told me he would help me dispose of Diamond—I should have bought a casket for her. For diamond had seen me through hard times. How could I forget or get rid of her? Well! He said he knew a guy who knew a guy who could buy her. So, I agreed, praying she would fall in good hands, as good as mine had been that had tenderly held her. Within a few days, he came to me with $50, claiming the deed had been done. I signed the title over to the man. Besides, at that time Diamond wasn't doing me any good. Later, I learned my *friend* had sold Diamond for $250. He pocketed $200 and gave me only $50. 'How unfortunate,' I thought, 'To have been robbed by one of my own!' It was a heartbreaking realization. This incident made me aware of the folly in men's hearts. Evil folks exist in this world and I must guard myself against them. I'll never forgive this man, for he preyed on my misery while I prayed for his kindness. This resolve went counter to edicts of my formative years. Father always preached forgiveness, but I let him down on this one and never to reverse course.

Little by little, I acclimated to life in America, one experience at a time. What a ride it was! I completed college in three years and moved to Columbus, Ohio. Just as I had been ill-prepared for life in a foreign land, my experiences in Wilmington were merely a child's play and paled in comparison to those I would face in my new city. What a life it *panned* out to be!

"You dim-witted African bitch," Sam Snackwell roared, frothing at the mouth. "Put my rent money right here," he said pointing his index finger annoyingly at the palm of his left hand. My eyes instinctively followed his finger in a slow and deliberate motion all the way to his ashen-frizzled palm. His finger nails were long and dirty and his white skin was alligator dry as though Sam had never heard of lotion.

Befuddled, I neither moved nor uttered a word, paralyzed by Sam's coarse language and uncouth manner.

"Who do you take me for," he snarled, spit spewing out of his mouth, "Rockefeller?" I shrug my shoulders, knowing my fate rested in a more powerful and revered force than Sam. As he spoke to me, he hissed. His hissing died to the annoying ring of my alarm clock that sounded louder than Sam's scoffing. Begrudgingly, I pulled my head from under my covers, prying my eyes open to steal a peek at the green neon light of my clock. It was 5.45 a.m. and I had to make haste lest I be late for work yet again . . .

My flat at Crystal Lake Apartment complex, my home away from home, had the semblance of everything wrong in my life. From its chirped and dilapidated brick walls, rusted staircases that creaked whenever I walked upstairs, an overgrown-weed and grass lawn that seemed to have made a do-not-mow pact with a lawnmower to an interior whose carpet was tainted brown as though subjected to a stampede. This tiny one-bedroom flat was roach infested that whenever I turned off my lights at night, I could hear a hissing sound as they congregated in my kitchen sink. And with a flip back on of my light switch, I could see a blanket of blackness rapidly vanish to the black hole from which they had come. This filled me with disdain, a crude reminder of the depravity of my life. There was no pesticide strong enough to be rid me of this pestilence.

There was nothing new in my flat. Because the complex was built in the early seventies, it still had its original amenities. The fridge was as old as Eve. Its door was stained with a giant smudge of black crud that no bleach could return it to its original sparkling white. Similarly, the paint on its handle was scratched and always felt rough to the touch. The interior light bulb was broken and unfixable. Similarly, inside the freezer, a large band of ice had formed leaving little to no room for storage. I didn't mind it; after all, I seldom had enough food to freeze. I cooked everything I bought and mauled it in a matter of minutes. I left nothing to warrant freezing. Compared to my parents' brick house in the village, with its orange tiles and a well-trimmed bougainvillea hedges, sky-blue painted steel gates that had an appearance of a prison, it had an opulence of affluence.

It was at Crystal Lake apartment complex where I met Sam Snackwell, my landlord, one late afternoon upon my return from work. This first encounter was not copacetic. He was a snobbish brute! I was standing in my living room with my back to the door when I heard a clipty-clop horse-like sounds of boots combined with deafening creaking sounds of stairs as someone staggered up. I didn't think much about it, but before I could make sense of it, my door flew open as Sam roughly pushed it without bothering to knock. It screeched noisily. Because I had forgotten to latch the door, I jumped in fright startled by his intrusiveness. I turned to face the door as in staggered Sam. He was a middle aged large chubby man whose mere presence in my living room, which was already small, made it become even much smaller. He was disheveled, haggard, and his hair was not only long, but also unkempt. Fumes of booze, from his breath, ambushed me as though the man had just bathed at Anheuser Busch Brewery off Busch Boulevard moments before his arrival. I could also smell the putrid odor of his body like meat gone rancid.

Common sense told me to run outside away from Sam, but I couldn't. As though he had read my mind, he roughly grabbed my right shoulder and sank his claw-like nails deeply into my flesh. I experienced pain . . . *real* pain. The harder he pressed, the painful it felt. Terrified and immobilized by his roughness, my nerves started twitching fretfully. Paralyzed, I could barely muster the courage to gaze into his eyes or beg for mercy for a crime, which I had yet to commit. Still, I stole glances at him from the corner of my eyes. All I could see was a pair of his beady red-hot eyes dulled with alcohol. There was no compassion in them. He viewed *all* . . . No, most immigrants, the luckless souls of the world, with disdain. I lowered my eyes to the floor following Mama Joy's instruction from my formative years to never stare at an adult eye-to eye. It was then I had this urge to draw a map on the floor with my big toe, but I refrained myself as I experienced a hollow feeling in my gut . . . *This* feeling enveloped and suffocated me. Soon, my knees began to shake fiercely. No violently. I knew Sam was watching me like a hawk. I felt his eyes piercing me from head to toe. I wanted to remain calm, but how could I? The man could see through me like one sees through a Windex cleaned window. Being a foreigner, living in his rat-hole paradise—Crystal Lake—I was afraid to speak. He probably thought I was illegal, though I hadn't told him my status. I wasn't, but my days for running out of status were numbered. Perhaps, to be fair to Sam, he might have suspected that much.

I felt another pinch in my shoulder, just a little pinch enough to remind me of Sam's presence in my midst. He applied more pressure, again and again and again as I continued to feel this dull pain in my shoulder. It increased by the minute the more he applied the pressure from dull to sharp. I was mad as hell as resentment crawled through me like a bad poison. No. I was angry! No man had ever roughed me in such a manner before. In fact, I wished Sam would strike me instead of pinching me to get it over with . . . whatever the '*it*' was, but he didn't.

Instead, he said, "Look here *Miss*," putting emphasis on the word '*Miss*.' Incensed, I raised my chin-up, stealing a glance at his red eyes. Still, there was no compassion in them . . . just emptiness. Suddenly, it dawned on me. How could he show me compassion?

He didn't even know my name. To him, I was, *Kwatasha*. Nobody. I was merely a bank from which he made monthly withdrawals without a deposit in the form of house repairs to my ramshackle flat.

"Your rent is three days overdue, again," he said reprovingly, with a smirk on his face. "Today is the day! You have to pay-up or else . . ." he said threateningly, a macabre smile forming on his face, revealing his buck teeth. I didn't move my eyes from him.

Feeble of hearted, I said, "I don't have your rent money," but Sam didn't hear me. He continued to stare at me contemptuously from head to toe.

"Today is only Monday. I won't get paid until Friday," I said trying to cover-up my shortcomings. The truth was I had misused my money from my last paycheck, meant for rent. Sam was not convinced. Being a landlord, he was accustomed to tenants' lies— *my* lie. I could see it in his eyes . . . His parents must have told him my *lie* from before . . . my delinquent habits, I mean.

Once again, Sam applied pressure to my shoulder, as my past intruded on my present to an incident I had long forgotten. It was the first time I had gotten in trouble with Mr. Snackwell Sr. On that day, I left work craving tea and bent set on making it upon arrival. I wasn't thinking about my rent whatsoever. Unfortunately, when I returned home, Mr. Snackwell Sr. was already there collecting rent from all his tenants. I knew it was end month, but I had not envisioned him being at my apartment at that particular time. For his routine for rent collection was as clear as day. He always came on the first day of every month, never the last. I had planned to go to the bank after my tea to deposit my check. I didn't like the unpleasantness of over drafting on my account. Even if I had deposited my pay, I knew the check I had wasn't sufficient enough to cover my entire month's rent. So, when he came to my apartment, he wasn't impolite like Sam. He didn't sink his claw-like nails into my flesh. He simply admonished me.

The second time I was late, he wasn't enraged like Sam. Instead, he said, "Young lady, I am going to give you *one* warning this time . . . You hear?"

"Yes Sir!"

He allowed an impressive moment of silence to elapse as his eyes scanned me. "You have one week to get everything in order . . . Do I make myself clear?"

"Crystal clear!" I said.

"Late fee charges are twenty-five dollars. Be sure to add that onto your rent check," he said emphatically, and bowed his exit.

"Yes!" I said, itching to salute him. I didn't

After Mr. Snackwell Sr. left, I felt sad as I calculated the additional hours I would have to pick-up at work to break even. Minimum wage was $3.35. The late fee he had imposed on me was much more than what I spent on food monthly. My diet comprised of macaroni and cheese—which cost $.25 cents—and ramen noodles. This was a significant change from my early college years when I looked at such meal with disdain. Sometimes, I modified my macaroni and cheese recipe by adding onions . . . and this made it very tasty! Occasionally, I added a vegetable for variety, opting for broccoli as the only viable option. My favorite collard greens were not always in the store when I needed it.

That was a few years ago. Come Friday, I knew I wouldn't have enough money in my account to cover my rent. There was a simple reason for this. I had gambled most of it on Ohio Lottery.

Gambling was an addictive poison of my adult life. I had never won anything significant to speak of for I was the unluckiest woman ever. Nevertheless, I played my numbers daily. I always hoped one day the pendulum would swing my way. It never did. Sometimes, to feed this addiction, I borrowed from friends. A few days ago, I borrowed some money from Charlie, my neighbor, hoping I would win. I didn't. What a mess!

I was reeled back to reality and Sam's presence when he tightened his grip around my shoulder again. Gradually, I turned my head and rolled my eyes-up to steal a glance at him again. It was obvious he was enjoying debasing me. A macabre smile still lingered on his face. Once more, I muted myself, as random thoughts emerged on my mind.

'Stay calm,' an inner voice said. *'He can't squeeze life out of your body. Neither can he squeeze money from you.'*

"You African bitches think America is *free,*" Sam said emphasizing the word *free*. "Well, it is not!" he added forcefully and breaking into an evil laugh . . . "Hee hee hee hee!"

'For heaven's sake,' I thought 'America was the land of the *free*, for the *free*, and by the *free!* A place where I could be *myself.*' Afraid of Sam, I dared not voice these thoughts. I thought about Emma Lazarus's poem, "The New Colossus," engraved on a tablet placed on the pedestal upon which the Statue of Liberty stood, particularly the lines that read:

Give me your tired, your poor,
Your huddled masses yearning to breathe free,
The wretched refuse of your teeming shore.
Send these, the homeless, tempest-tost to me,
I lift my lamp beside the golden door!"

As these thoughts floated on my mind, I didn't know what to do. I was the huddled masses. I was the wretched refuse. I, too, yearned to walk through the golden door, but I was neither here nor there!

Without thinking, I began to feel myself with the back palm of my left hand. I pressed hard on my face, feeling the warmth of my skin. 'Is it really me? Am I alive?' I wondered as I experienced Sam's pinch in my shoulder again.

Instantly, I had another lapse of memory, as I plunged farther and farther away from my present, from Sam Snackwell, to a strange world! No, not that strange . . . A familiar strange world. A safe welcoming world—my home across the ocean. I was not *alone*. I was sitting under the canopy of our gum tree with Mama Joy, my mother, when I saw someone approaching us . . . an elderly woman. 'But who was she?' I wondered. Being far from where we sat, her image appeared fuzzy against the sun's brilliant glow. As she drew closer to us, I still had a hard time remembering who she was . . . her name I mean. For the bank of my memory was frozen.

'Look harder dear,' a familiar voice whispered into my ear. *'Look harder! I know you know her. Yes! You know her.'*

I searched deeper into my recessed mind. Nothing came. Then, out of the depth of this fog, a light flashed. 'Yes, I think I might *know* her . . . I think I might *know* her!' I exclaimed with exhilaration.

'She is of kin!' a voice rung in my ear again.

But what is her name?

I sank farther into the thicket forest of my bygone days, searching for a sliver of hope for anything to clear the mystery of the stranger. 'I should *know* her name . . . Ahh! Yes. I know her. It was Grandma Tufroza, my mother's aunt, sister to her mother!

She was my grandma, too, as norm. By then she was drawing closer to Mama and me. Her back was curved forward like a bow against her stained white-maroon-checkered dress. She must have been over a hundred years old and had out-lived all her children. Her hands were stretched to her back with the tips of her brittle fingers clenched on her walking stick between her feeble hands. Her feet moved sluggishly as though rock weighted. I could see her much clearer now. She had no expression on her face. I squinted, my eyes so as to see her clearly. Her cheekbones were hollow and her old skin pruned up. The folds of skin on her brow were stacked together like bale of hay and glittered under the sun. Beads of sweat snaked down through each of these layered folds.

Right away, I knew Grandma Tufroza must have walked for an hour or so, up the steep Maragoli Hills to our home. I knew it because I had been up-and-down the jagged hills countless times. I wondered how she made it up the steep embankment, being almost a hundred years old! She must have strong bones, stiffened and hardened by the uncountable times of walking up-and-down the hills for years.

I turned my face from Grandma to Mama. Mama was doing something with her hands. She had a thin strand of grass between her fingers. She was playing with it. She was not looking at Grandma. No! She was toying with grass; she twirled it around and let it gently slide between her fingers. She did it several times, as if trying not to acknowledge her mother's sister, who was her mother according to Logooli lore. I knew she couldn't deliberately ignore her mother. She was not that kind of woman. Mama was sweet, kind, and giving. Gradually, she lifted her chin-up. There was a sparkle in eyes as Grandma drew closer to us. There was strangeness about her . . . I couldn't tell what it was. I examined everything she was doing. Maybe there was a lesson for me behind her act. Steadily, her lips parted, as though she was about to say something, but instead, she smiled. It was a deep breath of relief. By then, Grandma, was standing before us, her back curved with age was now more pronounced. She looked like a question mark! She was emotionless.

"Welcome home Mama," Mama Joy said as an impeccable smile appeared on her face and remained for a while. Grandma didn't say anything . . . she didn't even smile. She seemed pensive. I was certain she was going to tell us what she wanted. No, not wanted, but what she needed. That was it. For Grandma, it was never a want, but always a need.

"Welcome to our home," Mama Joy said jovially again. "Come and sit here with me Mama Tufroza," she added waving to her. Grandma jerked her strong frail body. She loosened the strong grip off her left hand off the walking stick. Slowly, she moved it forward, leaned on it, as a dark smile appeared on her face. She moved her feet sluggishly towards Mama, but she did not sit down. Instead, she bent forward, her already arched back doubling in curve even more than a bow.

As Grandma began to speak, her chin trembled. "My child! Oh my *Dear Daughter* . . . May our ancestors bless you tenfold! Without you I would be dead!" she said with a shaking voice. Aptly stated, Grandma was right. Many people in the Village would undoubtedly vouch to her stated remarks about Mama Joy. She was the fiery furnace of charity for her people.

"It is no problem at all Mama," Mama Joy said.

"Upanga, dear," she said without looking at me. Her eyes were firmly fixed on Grandma: "Could you please bring Mama Tufroza water to cool her parched throat?"

"Damn it! Why didn't I think of it first?" I mumbled to myself.

"What did you say?" Mama Joy asked.

"Nothing," I said. I was supposed to know these rudiments of our cultural etiquette. I did not need a reminder. 'I should have used *common* sense,' I thought.

Dying of shame, I dragged myself from the shade. My mind was racing in different directions. I wondered if Mama Joy was ashamed of me. Perhaps Grandma was too. 'I must redeem myself . . . Yes, I have to redeem myself,' I mumbled quietly determined to do the *right* thing. 'As soon as I offer Grandma her drinking water, I will march into the kitchen and prepare her a cup of tea. That was it. Mama shouldn't have to remind me of it. I was sure.'

When I returned with a calabash brim-filled with cold water, Grandma Tufroza and Mama Joy were still sitting under the shade. Two women. Two generations apart, their lives shaped differently. Grandma, in her youth, was a homemaker. Mama Joy, in her modern day living, was both a homemaker and an entrepreneur. Unlike Grandma, she juggled both roles. What a sight . . . of my two mothers! Grandma was indifferent and Mama had this innocent giddiness about her. Looking at her, I got this distinct feeling that had she a choice, she might have crawled into Grandma's bosom, just like she did with her mother when she was a little girl. Or just like I did when I crawled in her arms. My eyes popped with excitement as I began to intensively watch them. I caught a glimpse of Mama Joy's disapproving gaze, reminding me of my manners, which I seemed to have forgotten. I knew it!

Grandma knew it too! Feeling uneasy, I wanted Mama to reprimand me for staring at them, but she did not. Instead, she smiled, but I knew it was not a happy smile. If only she said, 'You ought to know better than staring at people . . . it is bad manners!' It would have made all the difference.

I bent my knees forward and handed Grandma the calabash of water with both hands. Mama laughed. I used both hands, not one hand in handing Grandma her water. That was good. Grandma accepted my offer with both hands too. Before she could gulp its contents, she took a sip, gargled and spat in the dust. She watched the dry earth swallow her spit until only a patch of brown earth remained. She repeated the process a couple of times. Then, without taking the calabash off her mouth, she guzzled its content and then boom, I heard aloud belch. I burst in laughter. Mama laughed. Grandma, too, laughed. Now I knew where I got my ill manners. It was a family trait. Grandma handed me back the calabash, and started rocking her body, back and forth, back and forth. But, she forgot to thank me! Where were her manners? Had it been me, Mama would have reprimanded me, but it was Grandma and she was old. I could see it, from the sable lines of her aging visible on her forehead. Mama exonerated her for ill-manners.

Without much ado, Grandma thrust her right hand into her bosom and pulled out a white-tainted cotton bag from her folds of skin, which had once nursed twelve lives, but now were listless and sagged. She gave it to Mama who gave it to me. Now I had two things in my hands. I knew what that meant. It was not the first time Grandma Tufroza had come to our home with that very bag.

"Why don't you get Mama some maize?" Mama Joy said to me in an endearing tone, not at all perturbed by the truth that Grandma was a regular visitor to our home. Why shouldn't she? Those who knew Mama's magnanimity would not see her giving hand any different. She was simply a good natured woman who came to the rescue of those who traversed her home. I had no choice, but accept the errand without question. That halted my immediate desire to make tea for Grandma!

Like Mama, I was not pained at all by Grandma's request. I simply resented having to crawl into the storage to get her maize. I disliked dust particles stealing stealthily into my eyes. Not just my eyes, but also my nostrils. Yes. The sneezing. Itchy eyes. Goodness, it was not pleasant to crawl into the granary. Sometimes, weevils crawled on my arms like spiders. Ouch, not pleasant at all. If I had courage, I would have asked Mama to do it herself . . . but that would be rude and not prudent.

I lowered my eyes to look at Grandma's bag. It felt warm. I was tempted to move it close to my nose. Very close. I wanted to smell it, smell the sweet sweaty-odor of her body. On second thought, I refrained myself. I knew Mama would see me. I didn't want her to say, 'What an incorrigible girl Upanga is! Smelling Grandma's bag like a she dog! *Tuffia*! Lord have mercy on her tainted soul!' As these thoughts raced through my mind, I wondered how many times the bag had been washed. No. I wondered how many times it had been hidden behind the folds of skin on her bosom. I couldn't sniff it . . . I just couldn't smell it. I began walking away from grandma and Mama, away from them to the granary. Away to . . . Hell! I didn't know where I was! Suddenly, I felt pressure in my shoulder once more as I tried to climb into the granary. I lifted my left foot to step onto the first step into the womb of the granary. Let it swallow me! Gulped me down like Jonah was swallowed by a fish. No. It was not a fish, but a whale. Everything was now moving so fast. I didn't know where I was or who I was. I was stepping onto the OTC bus hauling passengers to town, to the streets of Nairobi swarming with people like bees. Men and women.

In my mind's eye, I was setting foot into Central bank of Kenya. Before me, there was man whom I took to be the banker. An unfriendly fellow. His eyes were disarming, but his face was emotionless and had the semblance of a blank board. *'May I see your passport please,'* I heard the man's monotone voice say, *'You are going to college in the US . . . I see! School fees for your first year is paid in full! He slammed the stamp in my passport with the government insignia, hand wrote the amount of money I was to receive in American dollars--$ 18 to be specific—and handed me back my passport. Goodbye! Have a safe trip.'* I felt like I was in a horror movie . . . A dreamlike horror movie.

Then, my landscape shifted, but my mind remained a tussled squall. I moved my right foot onto a rolling step. Afraid of this moving monstrosity, nerves made my stomach muscles knot like banded steel. And then . . . there it was a giant entrance door . . . the Granary . . . the bus . . . the bank . . . No. It was not a bus, but a giant-metallic-winged bird that glides between the clouds. The nervousness of floating in the air caused my stomach muscles to tighten even more. New York! Here I come. America, here I come. Columbus! Here I am.

As I moved my left foot forward to get off the giant metallic bird, I experienced pressure in my right shoulder again. I emerged from the thicket recess of my mind to Sam's nails pressing harder and harder into my flesh. There and then, I knew when it was all over, Sam's nail-size marks would be engraved in my flesh.

"Sam Snackwell, you are hurting me," I said, gritting my teeth, but he did not pay me any attention.

"I have a mortgage to pay, you know!" I heard Sam say. I felt ashamed and embarrassed. Not for any major infraction I had committed, but simply because I had not paid my rent. I was a foreigner in the land of opportunity unable to make ends meet. No one had told me about the hardships of living in the land of the free . . . the land of opportunity. No one had warned me that American roads were not paved with gold, but laced with misery and hardships. No one told me I had to work day and night and fourteen hours in a row. No matter what I did or how hard I worked, all my efforts seemed fruitless. I wondered what Mama Joy would say if she knew of my struggles. Perhaps she might say, *'Upanga, you are not acting responsibly. I thought I taught you well! You are supposed to be independent and self-sufficient! You are not Grandma Tufroza. Grandma Tufroza was a hard working woman in her youth. I can excuse her begging for food on her aging, but not you. Sam is not our kin.'*

Sam had a terrible attitude towards foreigners . . . Not just any foreigners, but those of African descent. Although he was uneducated, he felt better than any black man regardless of his academic or financial standing. He had made this known to me many a times. He said we were stupid, filthy leeches bent on exploiting America's riches. He said most of us were criminals who belonged in the slammer. Never once did he consider our service to this great nation, employed in jobs American citizens disliked—like janitorial, mowing grass, picking fruits and vegetables on farms, or even my *own* job at a nursing home. Never once did he consider our contribution to the American economy. Never once did he think of us immigrants as victims of American employers who were bent on cutting costs by employing the poorest and most vulnerable newcomers and paying them meager salaries. Some of us immigrants, lived in his complex, worked, paid taxes, and paid their rent timely . . . I will make good of that on my part.

"Bitch! Did you hear me?" Sam said.

Mortified by his coarse language, I muted myself. No man. No woman. No person had ever called me that . . . that B—h word. I was not a she dog!

"I have a mortgage to pay," Sam said affirmatively. "If you don't have your rent, your *ass* is mine!" I was deeply offended by his language. With my ears attuned and without bothering to say a word, I looked at Sam contemptuously.

In my muteness, a deep feeling and new sense of longing enveloped me. I longed for Mama. I longed for her warm house. I longed for *our* warm home, even with Grandma Tufroza regular visits. I missed those. A home where foul language was as remote as snow on the equator. I longed for the azure skies of our village! I longed for the fresh scent of spring air, not the putrid odors of Sam's body like meat gone rancid. I longed for the simple and clear natural goodness! Unfortunately, I was in Columbus, Ohio. Its air polluted with fumes and, besides me, was Sam Snackwell with his Anheuser Busch odor. I wanted to say to him: "You son of a donkey, you can't speak to me like that! I have a home. I have a family. I am somebody." But my lips were heavy as though laced with glue. Sam wouldn't think I was somebody? I was certain my neighbor, Charlie Crabtree, wouldn't question my identity. I didn't care much about that any more . . . What people thought of me. I was somebody . . . *I am* somebody.

I was jolted back to my reality when Sam shoved me slightly, loosening his grip off my shoulder. I straddled backwards, nearly falling. He laughed sadistically . . . Haha, haha, haha, haha! I felt a sudden rush of anger mount within me like a bad poison again—twice in a span of minutes—as my ears began to burn. I moved my left hand to feel my right shoulder. There were giant marks engraved in my flesh.

"You aren't going to escape this time bitch." He fell silent for a few seconds. "I want my money," he said once more.

"I don't have it!" I finally said in a feeble tone.

"Don't you know this is not the Red Cross? You have until tomorrow. You hear me?" he said harshly.

"Crystal clear!" I mumbled, knowing profoundly well that I will not have his rent come tomorrow.

"Alright then, I will be back tomorrow and you better have my rent," he said walking out of my apartment noisily.

"Tomorrow! . . . Have my money or else . . ." he slammed my door behind him. The walls of my apartment rattled. Demoralized, I remained a fixture in my living room thinking about what had just transpired, an incident which had lasted only a few minutes, but seemed an eternity. I could still hear Sam's heavy clop of boots as he walked towards Charlie Crabtree's apartment, which was directly opposite mine.

10

After Sam Snackwell descended the stairs, I walked to my mullioned living room window, pressed my face hard onto the cold glass surface, and checked for any vestiges of him. I swept the stairs with my eyes step by step by step. There was no sign of Sam. Slowly, I shifted my focus in the direction of Charlie's apartment. I saw an arresting image of two dames locked in a long smooch. Charlie was nowhere in the vicinity.

Then, it dawned on me why Charlie hadn't opened his door when Sam Snackwell knocked. It had to be the girls. It was all clear now. I squinted my eyes in disbelief. For as long as I had lived, I had never seen two women intimate with each other the way those two were. Interestingly, though, in Charlie's living room. I rubbed my eyes, wondering if my sight had betrayed me. I looked again, but there was nothing wrong with my vision. In that one single moment, I felt I was witnessing something I had no right to witness. Had I become voyeuristic? I pressed my face once more on the window, and sure enough, they were still necking and kissing each other. Unbelievable!

Suddenly, my mind took flight to a conversation Charlie and I had many years ago.

"My sister-o-o," he told me. "I love women . . . Any woman. Brown. White. Any shade. You name them, I love them. I don't discriminate."

"Really?" I said.

"Women make my heart palpitate. They awaken the animal in me. Can you believe that?"

Charlie was so self-confident that he was often on the borderline of being obnoxious.

"If my mother were here," he said. "*My* sweet mother! She would say I take it after my father. He was a polygamist man, you know!"

"No. I didn't know that."

"He married seven women. My mother was his sixth wife. He sweet-talked her all the way from the comfort of her father's home to become his wife."

Then, Charlie broke into song, dancing, swaying his waist, and grinding hips to Prince Nico Mbarga's lyrics:

"Sweet mother I will never forget you, for the suffer way you suffer for me!"

He swayed his hips and breaking into a prolonged laugh.

"You don't believe me, do you?"

"No!"

"Why not?"

"Because you are bluffing. Women are not dumb."

I recalled, once more, another a minor incident at D.J. Prophets, a reggae joint in the Short North, where an unabashed Charlie sought to prove to me his prowess with women. The place no longer exists today, but it was the best reggae club in town. That night, the air was dense-filled with cigarette smoke and jam-packed with rowdy patrons, making it hard to have a decent conversation. This minor distraction didn't halt Charlie from expressing his views.

"Watch me in action," he said. "Look Sugar, watch me and learn! I guarantee you I am going to make that girl over there laugh. Not just laugh, but also dance with me."

"Where?"

"Right there," he said, pointing his finger to some lady who was seated by the bar. I moved my eyes to Charlie's pointing until they settled onto a blond woman. She was slowly sipping a glass of red wine. "You see, she is looking at me," Charlie said braggingly.

"I don't think she is looking at you! You are not the only man in this club." Charlie smiled. "She could be looking at someone else . . . I am serious, she could be!"

"No!" Charlie said affirmatively. "She is definitely looking at me. Look . . . You see she is even smiling at me. I know she wants me . . . Charlie Crabtree. As I said, I am going to make her dance with me."

"No, you can't," I said, convinced there was no way Charlie could make a fine woman as her and a stranger for that matter, dance with him. I was tempted to make a bet, but I refrained myself. By that time, the club was teeming with people. The DJ was playing Yellow Man's song, "Nobody Move, Nobody Get Hurt." There was laughter of people making merry as their bodies swayed to the loud music. Swirling cigarette smoke tainted every now and then with whiffs of Marijuana filled the air.

"You wanna bet?" he said.

"No, I don't bet, at least not yet."

"You are scared you'll lose," he said affirmatively.

"I am not afraid of anything Charlie!"

"You are too," he said, his lips drooping. "Tell you what, if I can't make her dance with me, I'll buy you a beer." I laughed at his silliness. "Seriously . . . I will buy you a Heineken. Colt 45. Old English. You name it. . . I will buy it!"

I looked at the pale-faced woman once more. She struck me as the kind who wouldn't fall for a character like Charlie. She was way too young for him, probably twenty-two or so. By comparison, Charlie was forty-five. She was wearing body-fitting-spandex blue jeans exposing her compact looking bums. I envied her. She was so attractive I was certain Charlie did not stand a chance. Her low-cut light-blue tailored blouse accentuated her appearance, revealing her endowed bosom. The more I looked at her, the more I was certain her melon breasts couldn't be real. Perhaps, she had silicone implants.

"Yes. That one," Charlie said, his face beaming with delight under the golden yellow lights of D.J. Prophets. I detected his lustful gaze. No. His mouth watered! Then, he quaffed his Red Stripe, swallowed saliva . . . tons of saliva, as though he had never seen a woman in his life.

"Watch me my Sister!" he remarked making ready to stand. "I wouldn't want to deprive you of a good spectacle," he added, walking off boisterously towards the blond woman. "Watch and weep girl!" No doubt, I intended to do just that, humor him a little.

"You are on!" I said with delight.

"Damn man! You can't be serious?"

"Trust me; it is fair game," he said, his back towards me.

As Charlie walked towards the lady, he turned his head back and winked his left eye at me. I made a gesture that was between a shrug and a nod, a kind of go ahead my brother shrug!

I was certain I would definitely get my Heineken, free of charge. My hopes were thwarted instantly as the woman, without any hesitation, turned to Charlie with a strange sense of familiarity. I wondered if Charlie had duped me. She smiled. Her small tainted buck teeth hard pressed against her thin lips glossed with red-hot-lipstick appeared. She tilted her neck, bent forward towards Charlie, revealing her lightly furrowed eyebrows in dimly lit light. Her contact cat-like-eyes darted in her eye sockets, microscopically inspecting Charlie. "Lucky dog!" I exclaimed. "There goes my beer!"

Feeling confident, Charlie pulled a high stool next to the lady. Once again, he turned his head towards me to ascertain my watchfulness. Sensing my attuned position, he smiled mischievously and then swerved back to his acquaintance, concentrating on his mission, while distantly the D.J. was playing *Sexual Healing*, Marvin Gaye's classic song:

Ooh, now let's get down tonight
Baby I'm hot just like an oven
I need some lovin'
And baby, I can't hold it much longer
It's getting stronger and stronger
And when I get that feeling
I want Sexual Healing
Sexual Healing, oh baby
Makes me feel so fine
Helps to relieve my mind
Sexual Healing baby, is good for me
Sexual Healing is something that's good for me

"How do you spell spot?" I heard Charlie say to the woman over the music.

"S.P.O.T." the girl said, with a surprised look in her eyes.

"How do you spell stop?"

"S.T.O.P," she said wide-eyed and smiling, exposing her tainted buck teeth again, perhaps browned from years of drinking too much coffee or smoking. Puzzled as though he didn't expect her to know how to spell, Charlie rubbed his temple. He was not winning.

"How do you spell silk?"

"S.I.L.K!" she said again, her eyes beaming in delight.

Damn! She got it right. Now for the kill, Charlie said, "What do cows drink?"

The woman did not respond right away. Then, with ease she said,

"Milk!"

Charlie laughed. The girl laughed. 'Phew!' I gasped. 'There goes my beer!'

Once again, I wondered if Charlie had duped me . . . Perhaps, he knew the woman all along. Maybe, Charlie had no intention of buying me beer after all. 'What a rascal,' I mumbled.

I was reeled back to my reality, to the two girls in Charlie's living room. The girls were still kissing each other, but Charlie was nowhere in the vicinity.

'Who were they?' I wondered. I had never seen them before. Not in our complex. Their lips were still locked in a serious French-kiss. What an unnerving view. Suddenly, an uneasy feeling came over me as though I was participating in some criminal act. My fit of voyeurism, I mean. While at the back of my mind, I felt I was stealing secrets that weren't meant for me. Secrets that were as strange to my sensibilities as dreams. In spite of this truth, my eyes continued to rove aimlessly in search for Charlie. From the girls to every corner of his apartment in view, but Charlie was gone. 'Maybe he was asleep," I thought.

In this disturbing moment, an inner voice egged me on, '*Look. Look. Look harder my friend!*'

I continued my quest for the elusive Charlie. I squinted my eyes, narrowing my focus towards the direction of the kitchen. I moved them up and down and sideways until . . . until I saw him. His body was crouched, with his eyes inspecting his wide open refrigerator. Inwardly, I wondered how he could let the girls frolic in his living room. My cultural biases hampered my rational thoughts. Perhaps Charlie had changed or become cultured in American ways. Charlie the womanizer, the symbol of African manhood, seemed like a different man than the one I met many years ago.

I saw Charlie reaching out for something in the fridge. 'Was it food?' I wondered. Not food, it couldn't be food. He hardly kept real food in his house. Perhaps Colt 45. Old English. Milwaukee Best. Bud Light. Miller Light, the addictive poison of his life. I was wrong! He pulled out a bottle of Zima, popped it open and gulped it! Gulp! Gulp! He guzzled it until the bottle was half-way empty. I imagined him letting out a disgusting loud belch. I moved my eyes back to the girls. They were no longer kissing, but holding hands.

I moved away from my window and walked to my couch while Charlie moved Zima back to his lips. I dropped my exhausted body onto my couch's artificial softness like a log, closing my mind away from Charlie and his girls . . . As my mind took flight to Sam Snackwell and his ultimatum, "Tomorrow! . . . Have my money or else!" I plunged into instant sadness. Who wouldn't?

I closed my eyes and disconnected the self from the world and everything, from Sam, from Charlie, from the girls. My mind raced thousands of miles away from Columbus, to my far, far away horizon—the sunny baked landscape of home—my leather strapped body airborne in the big winged bird soaring the blue skies ascending into the heavens. To the comfort of Mama Joy's home. To my father. To my brothers and sisters. To everyone. I plunged into my turbulent psyche, sinking farther and farther away . . . Away from my ramshackle apartment at Crystal Lake as I curled my body on my couch like a question mark. I remained lost in a world, which I had thought was destined to liberate me. Sadly, I had nothing. This truth ushered my sense of longing for home, *my* Vihiga home, and permeated every fiber of my being. I felt the giant bird glide with ease like a bird of prey aiming for a kill as it circled about Kisumu airport numerous times before its rubbery wheels kissed the tarmac. I heaved a sigh of relief happy to be in familiar territory. Oh . . . Yes! The beautiful sunrise above Maragoli Hills showered me with ecstasy.

The streets of Majengo swarmed with people. Men and women, young and old, boys and girls. I could hardly recognize them. Their bodies, brown-baked in the hot equatorial heat, dripped with sweat as they walked across the sunny baked Vihiga landscape dotted with large boulders. Some boulders laid as flat as a pool tables. Most folks walked barefooted with the skin on their heels encrusted with red clay. Others had cracks on their heels deep enough to swallow a pen. Women, married to farm hands who hardly brought enough food home to feed their children, loitered about the streets of Majengo like swarms of bees. Wide eyed, they searched and searched tirelessly for their daily grub. Others bargained with whomever they saw in the market, *matatu's* or buses along the Kakamega-Kisumu road, selling all sorts of commodities—boiled eggs, roasted or boiled maize, roasted groundnuts wrapped in pyramid-shaped newspapers, ripe bananas, or *sim-sim*. Their hearts' desire set on anchoring their lives, like an anchored boat against the tidal eddies of Lake Victoria . . . eddies of their turbulent present. Find their freedom. But freedom from what? Freedom from the clutches of their poverty. Freedom of choice. Freedom to speak. Freedom to live their lives in harmony. Freedom—their right and necessity. They desired and wanted freedom no doubt; swirl in the glistering hope of *Maendeleo ya Wanawake,* Women Progress. But what was wrong with a desire as noble as this especially for the weaker sex?

I, a question mark on my couch, drifted back-and-forth, back-and-forth from my present to my past and back to my present, my body dripping with sweat, like the mothers at Majengo. Suddenly, an image of Mama Joy and her friend fused into my present. The two women were sitting under a tree shade one hot afternoon enjoying a cup of tea. They didn't know I was there, eavesdropping on them, stealing their secrets. Mama's friend, of many years, worked as a secretary in the private sector. She had a lot of anger against the corporate world, and her heart ebbed her displeasure with society. Animatedly, she queried Mama on her duly noted dissatisfaction with society's blind eye turned against her plight and that of many other female folk. Her story enraged me. After she

left, I couldn't help, but make a poor attempt at writing a poem to
recapture the moment—
Have you ever been in a position
   in which you knew not
      where your daily bread comes from?

Have you ever been in a position
     where you were constantly taunted by persons in power
       but yet knew not where to go or to whom to turn?
        (See your husband)

Have you ever been coerced
    or thrust into a situation in which
       your bare existence depended upon your physical attributes?

Have you ever been in a position
    in which opening your legs
      is supposed to boost your ego
        up the ladder of social mobility?
         (Women are obedient, loyal,
             patient, and submissive to authority)

Then you know:
   a woman's plight is dismal:
   From sexual harassment
      (No! Means yes! They like it)
       low wages—
        (women's salaries are supplementary)
         to crude remarks—

(hire docile subservient women without self-
confidence, outspoken and self-confident women are troublemakers)
And you still think—
>   my place, our place
>   or my position, our position as women is easy?

I had no answers for Mama's friend. I returned to my wakefulness, in my apartment still curled on my couch, wondering how to escape my quandary. As I plunged into a new reality, a new landscape, I emerged to an addictive poison of my present life— gambling. The prospect of winning quick cash spurred my addiction. Not hard work, just the Ohio Lottery. I didn't take heed of the Lottery Announcer's Plea: "Please Play Responsibly!" Was I not a responsible player? I saw numbers flash on my mind. I tabulated them. Arranged them systematically, the best way I knew how, convinced that they would definitely win me the lottery. That week, the Mega Million Jackpot was one hundred and seventy-seven million. I was tempted! Oh, I was tempted . . . one hundred and seventy-seven million dollars sounded like a good chunk of change. Then, I began to dream real practical dreams. I could finally own an expensive car—maybe a Mercedes or Jaguar. Perhaps, I could own a big mansion with ten self-contained bedrooms, each with bathroom and a Jacuzzi lined with gold. A gold swash bidet toilet was a possibility too. I could have anything humanly possible that money could buy. I could bring Mama Joy and Father over for a visit. Possibly, Grandma Tufroza were she to be still alive. I imagined appearing on live TV to claim my Mega million winnings as my heart melted with joy aware Snackwell was now merely a ghost of my past . . .

11

Charlie Crabtree did not come to America shackle bound. He did not endure whip lashes on his back from a brutal master, or have roads carved on his back because of it, but was a victim of psychological castration from a colonial legacy of self-loathing. He had endured long hours, long weeks, long months, and long years of brainwashing. He was whipped into submission at the hands of his teachers determined to mold him into a perfectly civilized modern man. The sharp ear-deafening crackling sound of a ruler against his knuckles, which punctured his flesh until they bled for daring to use his native tongue, was hallmark to his total erasure of a past worthy of forgetting—the wild-savagery of his Africanness. So, he abandoned this life and immigrated to America ill-equipped for the challenges of his new life, but galvanized by dreams of hope for a better tomorrow armed with a degree in aerodynamics.

My path crossed his one night many years ago—in the late eighties—when I walked under the yellow golden lights of High street to the swirling smoke-filled, stale-smelling D.J. Prophets. A giant mural was carved on one side of its walls in screaming bright colors—orange, red, hot pink, brown—and hard to miss. The pub had long gone out of business, but the building still stands and is a great location for many other ventures. It was there our acquaintance began and blossomed into a permanent friendship, especially after I moved to Crystal Lake Apartment Complex. Henceforth, he became a dear friend and felt comfortable enough with me to divulge some of his secrets . . . secrets one wouldn't dare share with a priest at confession.

The first day I met Charlie, I had gone to DJ Prophets, the only reggae joint in town at the time, to listen to music. I loved reggae with a passion, having been introduced to it by a former classmate from Jamaica many years ago. Charlie must have noticed me upon my entrance. Right away, he approached me, determined to make my acquaintance. He paraded towards me with bravado, holding a Bud Light beer in his left hand and smiling broadly as though he and I were already familiar friends.

"Are you Nigerian?" Charlie said.

I didn't answer.

"Seriously," he added. "Are you Nigerian?"

I still couldn't answer, working-up a slow anger to his question and puzzled by his premature assumption. To me, in that moment in time, it seemed as though Charlie assumed, falsely of course, that the *only* Africans to America were Nigerians.

This was to the clamoring laughter of people above the blaring reggae music.

Not wanting to give up, he repeated the question after a brief interval of silence had elapsed.

"Seriously, are you Nigerian?" he said, as though I hadn't heard him the first time.

I looked at him with a frowning face veiled with hints of 'Leave me alone. Let me enjoy my music, will you?'

He didn't; instead, puppy-eyed, he gawked at me inquisitively. The glint in his brown eyes made me realize if I needed peace—any peace—I had no choice, but offer a response.

"I am afraid not," I said.

Faking a smile, he said: "You must be Senegalese then. That is it. You have the looks of a real Senegalese woman. *Masa* . . . with your high cheek bones, tall, and smooth faced . . . Not to mention your dark ebony skin, and those long thin braids. Aah! Aah! Fantastic. You have to be Senegalese then."

"What an idiot," I mumbled.

Charlie didn't hear me. He took a sip of his Bud Light beer to the deafening sound of another reggae song. It must have been Bob Marley's song, "Don't Worry about a Thing." Its lyrics were very soothing.

"Sorry to disappoint you again," I said. "I am neither Nigerian nor Senegalese!"

"I see," he said and fell into a deep silence. I took another sip of my drink, turning my eyes away from him. A waiter passed by asking if I wanted to buy another drink, but I didn't. She walked away to attend to another customer.

"Okay, I give up! . . . Do tell sister!" He paused, giving me a prolonged look. "Where do you come from?"

"Ding! Why didn't you say that from the start?" I said irritated. 'If only he knew I didn't like his company!' I thought.

"Humor me!" he said stubbornly.

"East Africa."

"Oh!" he gasped as though he had attained some astronomical revelation. "Why didn't I think of that? Nairobi, right?"

"I guess," I said, but he was wrong. Another misjudgment on Charlie's part . . . not all Kenyans come from Nairobi. My home was about eight hours drive away from Nairobi and 15 minutes' walk from where the equator crosses Kenya. I agreed with him, hoping he would leave me the hell alone.

"Are you alone?" he asked as though he was blind.

"What difference does it make?"

"Well, a lot."

"Uh-huh!"

"I could buy you a drink if you would let me."

"No thanks!"

"Just one drink and I won't bother you."

"I doubt it!"

"Please, I insist!"

"No!" I took a sip of my drink again.

"Alright then, but could you at least tell me your name? I promise I won't bother you again."

"I doubt that!"

"If you can't tell me your name, allow me to introduce myself!"

I looked on feeling trapped in this never-ending conversation and hoped it would end soon.

"My name is Charlie, Charlie Crabtree!" he added crossing his chest with his right palm. A broad smile flashed on his face, revealing his white evenly-lined teeth as though chiseled in place.

"I am Nigeria," he said prideful.

"I know that!"

"How is that?"

"You have the typical characteristics of a Nigerian!"

"True! True! Now that you know me . . . Pretty please, what is your name?"

"Upanga!"

"Don't you have a Christian name?"

"What difference does it make?"

"I am just curious . . . You must have been baptized!"

"No," I lied! My parents had baptized me in infancy long before I knew what it meant.

"You know the implication of that!"

"No!"

"Anything short of baptism connotes primitivism!"

"Says who?"

"Me . . . Any educated African ought to know that."

"What does that matter to you?"

"Any civilized African is baptized!"

"No!"

"Why not?"

"Mama calls me Upanga! My parents named me after my paternal grandmother."

"Okay Upanga," Charlie said with displeasure. "It is a pleasure to make your acquaintance!"

That night, Charlie did not keep his promise. I wasn't surprised. He pestered me all night long. Eventually, I left pledging to avoid him like a plague and if I ever ran into him again, I wouldn't give him the time of day. I was wrong. I ran into Charlie at the club time and again. Soon, Charlie turned out to be an okay guy whom I came to know and respect as a brother.

12

Besides being a womanizer, Charlie was a good-natured fellow. He had a big generous heart, a trait which most people found attractive—foreign students or African immigrants regardless of their country of origin—Kenya, Nigeria, Ghana, Cameroon, Tanzania. He never turned anyone away, even though he didn't have much to give. He took them in—come one, come all—those tempest-tossed souls yearning for a place to call home. He took them in indiscriminately. Unfortunately, because of the fallible nature of all mortals, some people, whom Charlie sought to help, took advantage of him. Some took the little he had for their own benefit, never giving thought to the sacrifice already made, or overextended their stay. Some even evicted Charlie from his bedroom to the living room. Being saintly, he remained that unmovable rock, steadfast and hospitable with his arms eagle spread ready to embrace all the huddled masses yearning to breathe free on freedom land. He reminded me of Mama Joy, who was a Mother Theresa of our village, and the embodiment of charity. Unlike Mama Joy, he never gave people a bag of maize or money, especially those on the verge of living on the streets. He gave them something more than money. He surrendered his personal comfort of home for their benefit. That was how Kobie, a Ghanaian brother, moved into Charlie's apartment seeking a week's refuge. What a farce! No one knew his story or from whence he came. He overextended his stay to one and half years.

When Kobie moved into Charlie's apartment, Charlie surrendered his bed for him, taking his couch for a bed. His mother must have raised him well, bound by the belief that it is improper for a host to let a guest sleep on couch while he enjoyed the comfort of his bed. Besides, Kobie had solemnly promised Charlie he only needed two weeks to get his life in order. Charlie agreed. Nothing could go wrong. Two weeks seemed a reasonable time. Unfortunately, two weeks came and passed. Kobie showed no sign of leaving and had no such intention. Two weeks turned into a month. Then six months. Before long, months elapsed into a year and more. Kobie remained an immovable enigma in Charlie's apartment. Charlie never complained.

He would tell me from time-to-time, "My sister! Mark my words, Kobie is leaving in two weeks!"

"Right!" I would say dismissively. "I'll believe it when I see it!"

It never happened! The guy had no intention to leave period! Who would give up the comfort he was getting for free. Before long, Charlie resigned to the reality that Kobie would never leave. He had chewed more than he could swallow.

Unlike Charlie, who was kind, warm, and a delight to be around, Kobie was not. He was a tall-slender man, moderately handsome, a braggart and as proud as a peacock. Never once did he fail to draw attention to himself. He was such a sharp dresser that his clothes were forever creaseless, ironed army-style, and matched to perfection. Naturally, he attracted such an entourage of women drawn to him not only because of his clean look, but also because of the sweetness of his tongue. He was, nonetheless, determined to convince all those whose paths crossed his to know, beyond reasonable doubt, he was *the* real deal! An African man, well endowed, and born of good stock, a bonafide stud muffin. He even bragged about it in the single's column of the local paper seeking a female companion. It worked for a while, but his bravado soon came to a screeching halt one afternoon in ways no one could have predicted . . . Not even Charlie, an incident that has forever haunted me to this day.

I had just returned home from work when my phone rang. I couldn't tell whom my caller was. Back then, we didn't have caller-id. If we did, I might have ignored picking-up my receiver to answer Charlie's call. I was doggone tired after working an eight-hour shift, therefore, I could have cared less to entertain his shenanigans. I picked up the receiver nonetheless as the neon light on my clock radio flashed 4:30 p.m.; already, the sky was heavily saturated with rain.

No sooner had I picked up my receiver than I heard Charlie's voice, "My sister-ooo! I beg . . . my sister-oo . . . You can't believe what just happened this afternoon!"

He didn't even say a simple hello.

"What? You didn't win the lottery, or did you?" I said.

Charlie never failed to play the Ohio Lottery. He once won ten thousand dollars, but squandered all of it on Somali women and booze. At least, that is what he said. He never even bought a t-shirt to remind him of his luck.

"No! I wish I had," he said. "It's much worse."

"If you didn't win the lottery, who died?"

"You always think of the worst. Don't you?"

"Not really!" I said.

"Nobody is dead . . . At least, not yet," he added.

Right away, my mind took flight to some of the undocumented immigrants in our community who had been rounded-up by Immigration and Customs and Enforcement—ICE—and had already been deported. Brother Marcelle was one of them. He was flown to his home country of Zaire with only the clothes on his back. He didn't last long. A years or two later, news came back that he had perished alone in a shanty-like hut. He had succumbed to a drunken stupor. There was no autopsy performed to ascertain the nature of his death for sure. And like a poof of dust, he was forever gone.

"What do you mean by that?" I said with irritation.

"I am getting to it!"

"If no one is not dead, what is it?" I said working up a slow anger.

Charlie was soundless, allowing a moment of silence to elapse.

"Get on with it before I lose my mind," I said, with my patience waned.

"Don't do that," he said. "I couldn't bear to have two people I know suffer from the same malady."

"What are you talking about?"

"It's Kobie, my friend . . . It's Kobie!"

"What is wrong with him?"

"He has lost his mind!"

"What? This afternoon? . . . Tell me you are kidding!"

"Why would I kid about something that serious?"

"What happened?"

"He lost his mind this afternoon. That is what happened."

"How did it happen?"

"Waah! My Sister—ooo--I couldn't believe my eyes!"

He paused for a second, allowing brief interlude of silence to pass and for me to absorb the truth behind his story.

"Let me tell you my Sister--oo," Charlie began to speak again. "Aah! Aah! The *bobo*," a term he used to refer to men, "spent most of his morning in the bedroom. He didn't eat. He didn't shower. He didn't speak to me. He didn't even answer the phone! He was just there."

"Did you try talking to him?"

"Of course I did. You know me my sister!" he added affirmatively. "I was lying on the couch watching T.V. when suddenly I heard the door fly open. I looked in the direction of the sound. He didn't even say a word to me, not even a simple 'hello!' He looked very glum."

"I see!"

"Right away, I knew something was wrong. He didn't look right! The *bobo* wasn't acting normal. He was mumbling to himself some unintelligible stuff. What a disturbing appearance! I asked him, 'What is wrong Kobie?' The *bobo* looked at me and shook his head vigorously—back-and-forth! Back-and-forth! I felt dizzy just looking at him."

"What then?"

"Before I could ask him anything, he sprang for the door." Right away, I tried to imagine Kobie dashing for the door.

"It all happened too fast . . . It happened too fast," Charlie added. His voice was full of regret. Still, I couldn't tell why this happenstance was odd.

"I ran after him!"

"What was wrong?" I said, imagining Charlie sprinting for the door.

"He didn't say," Charlie said with sadness in his tone. "Before I could make sense of what was going on, the *bobo* had walked out into the womb of the universe, under the open bowels of sky. I followed him as he descended down the stairs in haste as he disrobed like a man on a mission."

"What?" I said.

"Believe me!" Charlie said. "With each step he took, he threw his clothes behind. What a sight!"

"You don't say!" I said.

"What a strange despicable sight!" Charlie noted. "He nearly blindfolded me with them. Once naked, he thrust his strong masculine hands in the air and spread them out like an eagle in flight. His bare black body was such a sight: streaks of rain glided down his skin like rivulets. His hair had the appearance of dew-strewn grass."

'Wow!' I thought. 'How strange? There is a man determined to commune with Mother Nature under God's great tent of sky.'

"In a split second," Charlie said. "The *bobo* had forgotten proper social decorum . . . an unwritten law that deemed the human body indecent for public gaze. All the *bobo* could say was, 'The gods want me to bathe in their tears . . . Me Kobie!'"

I was dumbfound. I had no words to express my sense of shock.

"*Eiyaah*! My sister, can you believe that?"

"No!" I said, shaking my head as though Charlie see me.

'What a bizarre story!' I thought.

"To put an end to the *bobo's* foolishness," Charlie pressed on. "I grabbed him by his shoulders, hoping to pull his body towards mine so as to shield him from exposing his privates to public scrutiny, but the man was as strong as a horse. My hands slipped down his naked body."

I burst out into laughter, even though this wasn't a laughing matter. I tried to picture Charlie wrestling with Kobie.

"I tell you, it was as though he had acquired the strength of six people. Armed with this power from the Almighty, he fought me like a beast. I was not a match for him. A couple of other guys, who bore witness to the unfolding drama, came to my rescue. We tried hard to subdue him, but the *bobo* was a stubborn brute and as strong as the legendary Samson. We couldn't tame this beast. A neighbor, who had seen a naked black man dancing in the rain, called the police. They came right away!"

"My Sister-oo," Charlie added. "The *bobo* must have suffered a nervous breakdown!"

"He must have!" I said.

"There was nothing I could have done to save him," Charlie said with disappointment. "I missed all the symptoms of his illness!"

"I am sorry about your friend Charlie," I said when Charlie wrapped-up his story.

"Thanks!"

"Where is he now?"

"The police took him!"

"Will he go to jail for it?"

"I don't know. They might charge him with indecent exposure or disturbing the peace."

"I hope not Charlie!" I said. "I hope not. Thanks man for telling me about Kobie . . . I hope he is okay wherever he is!" I said and I truly meant it.

When my call with Charlie ended, all the energy in my body was waned. I sat in my living room in silence and distressed about the news. I didn't like the guy, but I didn't want him in harm's way. He reminded me of many other immigrants floundering in life, struggling to adjust to the American lifestyle, the American bounty, or a lack of it. He, a spec in the sea of despair. I also thought of many other Africans who had succumbed to the Kobie malady, like Papa, a Kenyan brother, who later took his life.

Days following the incident Charlie had narrated, I learned Kobie was committed to a mental institution for psychiatric observation. He was released after three weeks, only to be rearrested after a fortnight for assaulting a policeman downtown Columbus at the Greyhound Bus Station. That act alone, landed him in prison. One of the local T.V. channels carried a brief news segment on him. The anchorman had simply announced: "*A black male assaulted a police officer at the Greyhound Bus station downtown Columbus earlier this afternoon. He bit the officer and out of fear of contracting the HIV virus, the officer is undergoing testing!*"

Kobie's problems were testament of a life lived in turmoil and disharmony. A fragmented life. Days before the strange episode, he had been falsely accused of sexual harassment. No one exonerated him, but his psyche would forever be tormented by the charge. He retreated to the house, imprisoned himself in Charlie's bedroom. The loneliness of his alien existence on American soil was perhaps one of the root causes of his malady . . . Since his arrest, no one has heard of him again. He vanished from our midst as quickly as he had come and as though he never was. Maybe, he must still be in jail. Worst case scenario, perhaps dead! Whatever became of him—of his wretched life—has forever haunted me, a mystery of a life time; perhaps, save for the gods with whom he had sought to consort with on that fateful rainy afternoon.

For a while, Charlie didn't know what to do with Kobie's belongings. He packed them in a brown carton box and kept them in his bed room for years hoping he would return. He wouldn't dare throw them away . . . at least, not until he was evicted.

Since then, life for Charlie was never the same. He took to drinking incessantly. Alcohol, the worst of all intoxicants ever concocted by man, clouded his thoughts, making him lose the moral compass of his life. Just as much as it had clouded Sam Snackwell's judgment, alcohol obscured Charlie's decisions countless times, and many more Charlies to come. He once jokingly said when his mother was expecting him, she drank Guinness Beer . . . some doctor had advised her to do so. *'Beer is good for the baby!'* No wonder Charlie was an excessive drinker, a validation he used in justifying everything wrong in his life.

13

Three hours later, I was startled from sleep with a loud ringing sound of my telephone. I didn't reach out for it right away. I let it ring a second and a third time, angered by its deafening and intrusive sound. "I should have turned off the ringer," I said grumpily, fumbling with the receiver and hoping it wasn't Sam Snackwell calling.

I moved the receiver to my ear. "Hello!" I said

"My sister!" came a familiar voice on the end of the line. "It is me, Charlie!"

"Oh! Charlie," I said sounding groggy. "How are you?"

Wide-eyed now, I was angered by Charlie's disruption of my rest, wishing I had feigned being asleep. Knowing Charlie, though, he wasn't the kind of man easily dismissed. I knew my effort would have been wasted on him.

"Okay I guess. How about you . . . Are you alright?" Charlie said. There was an earnest sense of concern in the sound of his voice. It must have been something in my tone that prompted his question.

"Of course I am okay . . . I was just taking a catnap."

"That is unlike you to be in bed at this hour of day."

"Who said I am in bed? I was simply taking a *nap* . . . There is absolutely nothing wrong with me," I said between yawns. "I must have worn myself stupid earlier today."

I was expecting Charlie to say something, but he didn't. Maybe he had nothing to say. A brief moment of silence followed. The truth of the matter was that Sam's threats had greatly unnerved me, stirring anxiety deep within me. Fears of being evicted, hung upon me like cold molasses.

When he spoke again, Charlie rumbled on about the two dames I had seen earlier on in his apartment.

"My Sister," he said. "Let me tell you what happened to me last night!"

"What happened?" I said excitedly, with a changed attitude.

"You won't believe this," he said. "Last night I went to this African Night Club . . . You know it . . . I mean Club Zanzibar off Morse road."

"Aha! Yes . . . Yes!" I said. I had heard an ear full about this club from my other acquaintances. I hadn't visited it and had no intention of doing so. I had given up the night life, opting to focus my energies on work and school.

"What happened when you got there?" I said eager with anticipation.

"Let me tell you my sister-oo! The club was jam-packed with young men and women from Tanzania—at least the majority were—and a few West Africans. Eeh! Eeh! Eeh . . . I beg . . . Tanzanian men were exquisitely dressed to kill in their brand named, sporty and superb tailored attires: Tommy Hilfiger. Fubu. Jnco. Southpole. Plugg. Giorgio Armani. Visage. Calvin Klein. Christian Dior. Any designer brand you can think of, they had it on. I could have counted those who were casually dressed like me. I bet most felt too good for Old Spice. For some, the odor of their bodies was so overpowering I thought they had dipped themselves in either Eternity, Obsession, Drakkar, or Acqua Di (GIO). Most pranced around exuding an aura of ultimate importance. These scents fused with the dense cigarette smoke, making the air in the club dense and musty."

"Really!" I said. "Do tell."

"It was insane!" Charlie explained. "The D.J., a Kenyan fella nicknamed Othorongongo, was playing an array of African music: Ndombolo, Reggae, and some American hip-hop. Then, out of nowhere, emerged two African sisters. You should have seen them!"

I listened in silence as Charlie went on excitedly with his story.

"The girls were deftly dressed in tight-spandex jeans that revealed the contours of their bodies, curved to the T. Their faces were heavily glossed with what I took to be Fashion Fair Soufflé makeup to disguise any of their imperfections, if they had any, and radiated in the soft yellow lights of the Club."

Charlie fell silent for a second as though allowing time to absorb his narrated event. I, too, remained quiet.

"No sooner had they set foot inside, than they held all of us in a hypnotic gaze," Charlie said. "Men and women! I, too, was held captive by their beauty. I bet they could feel some men undressing them with their eyes . . . I beg! They couldn't do a damn thing about it."

Charlie paused for just a fraction of a second to catch his breath. I could feel the excitement in his tone. I pictured what he must have done when he saw the women as I recalled the first time I met him at D.J. Prophet. I could see him, in my mind's eye, brushing his short kinky hair backward, looking at himself admiringly. I could see him licking his chops, knowing only too well that if he didn't get any one of the women, his name wasn't Charlie Crabtree. I could see him walking to the girls determined to use his silly spelling tricks to make their acquaintance, like he had done many times—'How do you spell the word spot?'

"My sister," Charlie said. "You could have heard a pin drop were it not for the loud voices of Kofi Olomide's band singing *Effrakata*—one of their famous songs. The sound of it was blustery and deafening through the speakers. As the song came to an end, Bob Marley's classic *No, Woman, No Cry* came on. Reggae enthusiasts rose from their seats, made it to the dance floor, and began swaying their hips to Marley's soothing voice and cool rhythms.

The girls, who were peach ripe and reminded me of a succulent crimson tomato, too, made it to the floor.

"I walked towards them stealthily and steadily. When I approached them I said, 'Good evening Pearls of the Nile!' Charlie paused for a second.

"The girls looked at each other my sister and smiled," he said excitedly. "And that was a good sign! A real good sign. As though they had read my mind, they made room for me to join them, sway to the seductive lyrics of Marley.

No woman, no cry
No woman, no cry
No woman, no cry
No woman, no cry

"I was on cloud nine. Who could have imagined the girls would have danced with me . . . Me, Charlie Crabtree. When the song came to an end, we made our way to an empty table, sat down, and quickly began to get acquainted. The girls were Somali. I ordered them a couple of drinks and the next thing I knew, the girls were here with me . . . in my *crib*," he said putting more emphasis on the word *crib*.

"What a story Charlie!" I exclaimed. "Are you fibbing me?" I said pretending I had not seen the girls in his living room earlier that evening.

"No!" he said resoundingly. "But get this! What was odd," Charlie continued, "The girls had no interest in me. Me, Charlie Crabtree! If you know what I mean!"

"Get out of town! How come?"

"Ask me another," Charlie said jokingly. Not that he wanted me to take him literally, but that is exactly what I did.

"So, why did they come home with you if they were not interested in you?"

"Beats me! We got to talking and drinking some whisky and before we knew it, the night was spent."

He paused for a moment and emitted a prolonged sigh. "All along, I just thought when it was all over, I would get one of the girls interested in me . . . You know! Unfortunately, it turned out the girls were same-sex appreciators!"

"What do you mean?" I said feigning my ignorance.

"These are girls who like other girls."

"Wow!" I said, feeling sorry for Charlie.

I knew from our numerous conversations, Charlie struggled to understand same-sex relationships. He was traditional that way. I was no different. I, too, was traditional, never having grown up or seen same-sex couples. The idea, to me, was still alien and wasn't a part of my sensibilities. There was no word for such relationships in my Logooli language. It may have been a taboo among my people. I don't know if Charlie knew the girls were gay when he invited them to his home. He once joked he was a stud muffin capable of transforming a gay woman into a viable heterosexual.

"I tell you my Sister! The experience of having the girls in my living room, necking and kissing each other was something else. They didn't even feel ashamed or embarrassed to see me watching them."

"So, what did you do?"

"I excused myself, left them in my living room and went to my bedroom to sleep. Two hours later, when I returned, they were both sound asleep on my couch, their bodies locked in a tender embrace."

"I wonder why they chose you," I said.

"Eeh! You know me my Sister . . . I am a good guy!" he said in a firm braggadocios tone.

"I know!" I said and meant it. Charlie may have had other issues in life, but he was a good-natured fella and good fellas are hard to find.

After unburdening his heart, he added, "My sister-oo- if only I could understand women!"

I burst out in laughter.

"What's funny?" Charlie said irritated.

"Men all over the world have been trying to understand women for centuries," I said.

I thought of telling him, 'Brother, stop trying to understand an impossibility!' Or what Mama Joy always said about women. 'Women are demons who make men enter hell through the gates of paradise. They are supposed to be nurtured, not *understood*. It's hard to understand an enigma,'" but I changed my mind. I knew he wouldn't understand. Instead, I said, "Charlie, women are mysterious beings. That's their nature . . . it is who they are. No. Who *we* are and no different from men in nature and diversity."

When my conversation with Charlie ended, my mind raced back to Sam Snackwell's visit to my apartment hours earlier. I was nervous that come tomorrow, my eviction would happen. Because of it, I could barely sleep. I could see *my eviction* staring at me as I recalled an image of a dispossessed mother I had seen one dreary afternoon. Her sullen frame was forever etched on my mind.

I was driving home from work on Dublin Granville road, when suddenly I had a craving for arrow roots. Changing course, I turned right onto Cleveland Avenue heading south to Asian Market, an oriental store, where most African immigrants bought exotic produce from their countries of origin—quail, yams, arrow roots, cassava, potato or jute leaves. Such produce weren't found in supermarkets like Kroger, Meijer, or Giant Eagle. Only oriental stores carried them, but they were rare and expensive. Once in a while, to pacify a nostalgic craving for my homeland, I splurged on these delicacies. That was why I found my way to Asian Market with ease. Cleveland Avenue was hardly congested. I arrived at the parking lot within no time, parked my car, killed my engine, and walked into the store. I was greeted by a rapt gaze of a petite Asian woman, but she appeared disinterested in my entrance. I knew exactly where the arrow roots were stocked, and without looking at anything else, I headed straight for the big wooden case where they were stored. I picked one mid-sized tuber, and walked back to the counter. The petite woman rang the cash register and completed my transaction without saying a simple hello or making the customary small talk, 'Did you find everything you needed?' I didn't mind, but wished there was another alternative for getting international produce. I vowed if such store opened, I would never return. Her attitude wasn't good for business.

I left momentarily, hopped into my car, my gold diamond, and cranked the engine. It purred on the first click. I pressed the gas pedal, shifted the car into gear, and released my foot from the break. The car glided off the parking lot. I turned right heading north on Cleveland Avenue until I got to Cook Road. I veered to the left and then, after one block, I swerved to the right onto Walford road. I was just one block, south of Morse, when I saw it all. A mother, an elderly woman, slightly younger than my own mother, gazing at her belongings tossed out of her apartment like useless garbage—chairs, dining table, her two brown couches, clothes, dishes, and everything of value to her, but no one else, dispersed in the street like mushrooms on a hill.

The woman was fighting her evictors like a rabid dog gone crazy, while her evictors, with iron-clad hearts, were determined to see their task come to a successful completion. They showed her no mercy. She, a luckless soul, mourned despondently. A few spectators who had gathered to bear witness to the sad saga watched dispassionately not daring to intervene. I, too, watched. Without thinking, I pulled over within earshot of it all and continued in my watch so as to not clog traffic. I didn't turn off my ignition. Amid it all, the bowels of sky opened-up in a slow trickle of drizzles. Soon, these drizzles morphed into a steady downpour, drenching the poor woman. I watched her with curious intensity. Her large sad brown eyes were to her 'door' as her frail body yielded to God's unforgiving punishment. Then, her teeth began to chatter like clinking castanets while her voice as frail as glass could barely clamor her defense. Muted, I sat in my car, paralyzed by her pain. She, too, was paralyzed like a butterfly under a glass unable to escape her tumultuous present. I wanted to cry for her, my humanity, share in her pain because her reality was my impending reality, but I couldn't. My tears couldn't right everything that was wrong in her life, or bring a roof over her head and neither could they right my wrong. It was during this time that my thoughts, without my consent, took flight from my present and tumbled down and down, down further away from my now. Down and down to my entrenched past as though this very past was like a fast-paced motion picture . . . all the way to Mama Joy. I was certain were she here, she would have known exactly what to do for this poor woman, she the concomitant female power and Mother Theresa of Kerongo. Were this stranger in her midst, she would have taken her into her home, *our* home. I wasn't like my mother, even if my heart was willing. I had nothing! I had absolutely nothing! Puppy-eyed and filled with remorse, my lips fell half open as I muttered, 'I have nothing. Come tomorrow, her fate would be my fate!' Instantly, I felt like a dolphin swimming among sharks, with Sam Snackwell as one of sharks.

I saw no way out of my quagmire. So, I squeezed my eyelids tightly shut as though pushing the woman's image out of my mind and determined to stop my conscious mind from slipping into scenes from my past. It was useless. My mind continued to churn on in the darkness of night. 'What a torturous tempest-tossed sleeplessness night!' I thought. For once in my life, I wished I had sleeping pills to take my mind off things. I had no such luck. When sleep finally came hours later, I hardly noticed. It simply snuck-up on me like a thief in the middle of the night and took over my body, mind, and soul. I ceased to be, but was soon startled from slumber by the loud deafening sound of my alarm clock. It was six in the morning.

I threw my covers off and dashed to the bathroom. Thank goodness I lived alone. I turned on the tap and quickly undertook my morning ritual. Brushed my teeth. Shaved my armpits. Quickly showered. Towel dried my body. Got dressed. Took an admiring look into the mirror. Put on my borrowed face—forehead dabbed in my soufflé make-up foundation. Delicately arched my eyebrows. Glossed my lips in purple lipstick. Tied my synthetic braids into a ponytail. Within fifteen minutes, I was out and ready for the world. No coffee that morning. I would have to grab a cup on the way. Phew! What a life!

Once outside, I could see the early signs of spring. The white coat of snow had melted away exposing the bareness of trees. Their branches were bursting with new life evidenced with their tight-budded tips. I knew soon and only too soon, the buds would blossom into blooming merriness. The air was pitilessly raw and I could feel it to the bone because the morning was pale-washed with a misty fog and cloaked the earth like a blanket. I made haste in opening the door to Diamond, whose locks were almost inoperable, a result of many years of usage. I pulled hard on the knob until its metallic latch swiftly flew open. It emitted such a deafening screeching sound it hurt my ears. Oof! I sighed.

Right foot in first, I leaned forward towards the steering wheel, and gently pushed the key into the ignition. Left foot in second, I scooted my bottom onto my gray tattered synthetic chair. I felt its rough edges snag my pants, but I didn't care. I turned the key to the right and attempted to start the engine. It rattled, emitting a choked growling sound like an old man suffering from a phlegm-laden cough. I wondered if it would die, a threat which scared me a bit. This scare made me wish I had a BMW E60 5 series car, a dynamic drive, a car that delivered more agility for driving than anything I knew. A car that wouldn't throttle at the turn of a key, or cough like an old man struck with tuberculosis. I pressed hard on the gas pedal of my Civic. The engine rattled again, nearly stalling. 'Oh, God, please don't let her die,' I kept on saying. When the engine finally sparked, I was so relieved I could have jumped over the moon.

Out of habit, I turned on my radio and switched the dial to 90.5 FM, but I barely listened to it. With my right foot on the break, I shifted Diamond into reverse gear, and gently released my foot off the break as she slowly glided out of my driveway. I shifted the gear into drive, and accelerated, but going easy on the gas pedal. She moved smoothly out of Crystal Lake Apartment Complex to a service road. After 0.3 miles, I turned right onto Proprietor road and made an immediate left turn onto Dublin Granville road east bound. I watched familiar landmarks appear and fly past me: McDonald's. Wendy's. Burger King. Kentucky Fried Chicken. Staples. Shell gas station. When I got to the intersection of Dublin Granville road and Cleveland Avenue, I took a right turn southbound. After a couple of blocks, I took another right onto Teakwood to St. Grace, my place of work. Once in the parking lot, I let the engine idle for some time while I took a deep breath garnering courage to walk into the doors of St. Grace. Facing the grouchiness of my clients and Joyce's overbearing willpower over mine. I needed grit. The engine of my Civic purred softly as I silently watched the wind blow mist against my windshield. Beyond this windscreen and into the vault of sky, the sun struggled to peer through the hazy clouds. Above the rooftop of St. Grace's main building, whiffs of smoke stole stealthily through the chimney and melted into open space. This was a crude reminder of the morning chilliness. I took a deep breath, killed the engine, and pushed the door open. It screeched as always. I ground my teeth in disgust. As I got out, the air was still cold and I could feel its chillness against my exposed skin. This was just a minor distraction.

I made straight for the giant glass automated doors of St. Grace. No sooner had these doors flown open, than I was struck by the musty and nauseating odors of St. Grace. This was nothing compared to the outside freshness. The interior air was stale—hospital-like smell—a mixture of different kinds of medication, food, urine, puke, and anything deemed repugnant. These smells exuded in me a gut-retching feeling of wanting to gag or flee from the very place that gave me my livelihood. 'I have no choice,' I consoled myself. 'In a few years, upon completion my Master's Degree from The Ohio State University, I was certain I would no longer work in a Nursing home. Therefore, as long as I was still in school, I resolved to work as a nurse aid.

It was approximately 6:45 a.m. when I arrived and still had fifteen minutes to kill. I was ecstatic I wasn't late for work. I had made solemn promise to myself, from my younger years, to always keep time no matter what. This was a lesson I learned from my father many years ago. My father valued being on time more than anyone I knew. He exercised it daily. A one-of-a-kind fella. Time for him was never relative. I recalled how he once left Mama Joy behind because she wasn't ready on time for a planned trip to a church function to Kakamega. She was still busy giving us instruction on what to do in her absence when we heard Father start the car. Without calling her or sending one of us to fetch Mama, he put the car in drive and rolled out of our gate. Mama came out in time to see the tail end of the car amid swirling dust as his tires sliced the gravel. He didn't look back when she called after him to stop. It was kind of mean for him to have done that to Mama. I never forgave him for it.

Father didn't and couldn't understand Mama's perception of time. Her time wasn't fragmented in seconds, minutes, or hours the way Father saw it. Everything she did happened because it had to be done, in spite of time. Before that day, I had never understood what Father meant whenever he told me, "Upanga, don't you ever forget time lost is forever gone. Don't waste *it* on idleness. Idleness is the root cause of most of the vices you see in this village!"

That morning, Mama wasn't wasting time on idle chatter. She was doing what she was supposed to do as she routinely did, hallmark of a good mother. Father was too impatient to wait. When he returned home that evening, he made no apology for his behavior. And this was a lesson we all took to heart.

My boss, Joyce Olson, was no different than my father. She had his attitude towards time and was a slave driver at best. I headed straight for the kitchen determined to make a fresh cup of coffee before Joyce's arrival. All the while, I thought about her views of most of us, her employees—new immigrants on American soil—whose perception of time was temporal, not linear the way Americans saw it, fragmented in seconds, minutes, and hours. Because most of Joyce's staff was of African origin, Ghanaians being the majority, she knew *they*, except me, were terrible with time. Albeit their tardiness was for the same reasons as my mother, but once they began their shift, they were workhorses. Joyce always said, "I tell you my friend, if only Americans would take pride in working in such places, I would fire all you all!" I jokingly told her, "I wouldn't mind the firing!" I didn't mean it, of course, but it felt good to say it. I hated my job with a passion, except I needed the money. It paid my bills. Given what we had to do, I understood why Americans hated the job. They had choices I could only dream of. If I could have traded places with them, I was certain I would make a similar choice. That was a fact!

Before I emigrated from home to America, I had never envisioned working in a Nursing home. How could I? I had never heard of such facilities. In my Kerongo Village, there were no nursing homes. We took care of our elderly. Handicapped folks didn't fare as well. Some were shunned because of their disability, but not the elderly. They were our prized jewel. There was no monetary value attached to their care. It was given freely with love and joy. Yet, on American soil, I was busting my tail off for a meagre salary. The work was strenuous. I derived neither joy nor pleasure from it. I wondered if my fellow immigrants felt the same way I did—those from Africa, in particular, and Mexicans, immigrants who sacrificed their lives crossing a treacherous border to make a buck. They, too, like me, worked in places most Americans hated with a passion—gutting fish, picking produce, working in construction, or cutting grass. For me, being a care giver wasn't an ideal profession. No. This wasn't *my* profession. It was a necessary derailment from where I wanted to go in life. For this reason, I kept my eyes on the prize—to complete my college education. No matter what. The only Americans I worked with held supervisory positions . . . like Joyce!

Fortunately, Joyce was a different breed of American. She was a good-natured woman whom, with a push of a button, would dash in a flash to aid any of her subordinate staff needing assistance with a client. She was a workhorse all right. She made sure her nursing home maintained its 'pristine' standards, but all her efforts were not enough to be rid of the place of that awful institution smell. She was also a very strict boss and nearly worked us to death much like a drill sergeant. This was her only mean streak . . . her go, go, go, attitude. One wouldn't dare take a moment's rest on her watch without being reprimanded not even a sip of water to quench a parched throat! No wonder a majority of her staff were Africans and most came with a host of problems—some perhaps didn't have a state identity card or social security numbers to warrant their gainful employment. I couldn't tell you who they were because I never asked. No one did. It was safe that way. For this reason, they took on any job that fell into their lap. Their meagre salary was no deterrent. They, too, like me, lived in dilapidated houses, like my rat-hole apartment, unfit for humans.

That morning, I hustled to make my coffee, aware that by 7:00 a.m., Joyce would be there. Without doubt, she would expect me to be on my wing, catering for the needs of my clients: Betty, Cherry, Bill, Sam, and Jerry. As an aid, my responsibilities were simple. I didn't need a degree to execute them: Check the chart every morning for my duties for the day. Check those clients with doctors' appointments so as to get them ready in a timely manner. Bathe those who needed to be bathed. Assist those who needed assistance. Ensure all clients were well fed. Make certain the clients' beds were neatly made and sheets were changed. Documentation of a chronology of each client's daily activities was paramount. One could be fired for failing to complete this process of the daily routine.

I put the coffee in the percolator and watched it drip—drop-by-drop! Drop-by-drop! Within no time, I could smell its fresh aroma. I closed my eyes inhaling in this freshness, wishing I had ample time to enjoy it. I opened my eyes, walked to the fridge, and reached out for a gallon of milk to add to the coffee. All the while, I kept on thinking, 'Surely, nothing could distract me now.' I poured a little bit of it in a mug, walked to the microwave, opened it and put the mug inside. I set the time—one minute and two seconds—enough to warm the milk. As I waited patiently for it to heat-up, I peeked at my watch to see if I still had time to enjoy my coffee, a half a mug at the minimum once ready. Only five minutes were left before my shift officially began. Seeing that, I knew Joyce and the other employees on my shift would be in soon. Although I knew I was running out of time, I still had hope I had time to pacify my caffeine addiction. I had to have it . . . my coffee, I mean . . . really!

Phew! What could go wrong now? No sooner had I heard the beeping sound of the microwave than I hurriedly reached for the mug and filled it with steaming coffee to the brim ready to indulge myself. I turned off the coffee pot, picked-up my cup, and walked to the office where I sat. Sighing contentedly, I closed my eyes and savored the coffee's aromatic flavor and freshness, loving every moment of it even though for a brief moment. I was oblivious to everything around me—the putrid smell of the Nursing home, sounds of shuffling feet as workers arrived for their morning shift, voices of clients who were already up needing assistance. I smacked my chops after my first sip and sighed merrily thinking I still had plenty of time before my shift began.

When Joyce walked into the office, I hardly heard her soft footsteps against the hard wooden floor. I was only startled by the sound of her voice calling my name, "Mary! Mary! What are you doing?"

I didn't answer. In my recessed mind, I wondered who Mary was! It wasn't me.

Having changed my name several years ago, from Upanga Kagai to Mary Upanga Kagai, I sometimes forgot my assumed name. I was often angst, to my wits end, whenever people mispronounced my name, Upanga, which made my name change inevitable. I was still getting used to this new identity. Only Mama Joy and my siblings still called me by my *true* Logooli name.

"Mary!" I heard Joyce's voice once more. "Weren't you supposed to be checking on Betty this morning?" I opened my right eye, stealing a peek at her. Her eyes were sharp and piercing, only duty bound! There was no love in them. A part of me knew I ought to have started my duties, but the joy of sipping on my coffee—one more time—superseded my rational thoughts. I only wished to gobble-up my coffee, but out of fear of burning my tongue and throat, I refrained myself.

"You know Betty has an appointment at 10:30 a.m.," she added. Blinded by the desire to satiate my caffeine addiction, I had forgotten to check my chart upon arrival so as to know which clients had scheduled appointments.

"Mary, you better hurry-up!" she added abrasively.

I pried my eyes open and stood up abruptly, and fixed them on my coffee mug. Steam spiraled from it into open space and vanished.

"She needs to get ready right away," Joyce barked.

"I'll get to it!" I said with my back to her.

"You better. She is a slow eater . . . You know!" she added. "The sooner you get her ready, the earlier I will be able to take her to Doctors North Hospital."

"Okay Ms. Joyce," I said. When I checked my watch again, I was surprised it was five minutes after seven.

Seeing that, I bolted out of the office, leaving my half-finished coffee on the table. 'I'll come back for it in due time.' I mumbled, but this pronouncement was only false hope. By the time I finished the first leg of my morning, the coffee wasn't fit for the mug in which it was, having lost all its flavor and taste.

Betty Snyder, my first client, was a bilateral amputee and weighed 315 pounds, a little over twice my weight. I had not planned to begin my morning with her, but I had no choice. She could do seventy-five percent of the work for herself, like washing her body, brushing her teeth, or putting on her clothes. Oftentimes, she cleaned herself because there was nothing wrong with her upper body. I was tasked to assist her in getting out of bed, changing the sheets, and making her bed. Occasionally, whenever she was in a bad mood, she obstinately refused to do any of it. What a humbling and strenuous experience!

When I walked in her room that morning, I was suddenly struck by its staleness and a repugnant odor, of sweat, fecal matter, and urine. I could only imagine what might have happened to her on the previous shift. Obviously, someone from the third shift must have forgotten to aid her in getting out of bed to the bathroom. That was all she ever needed—a simple show of human courtesy and kindness.

"Good morning Ms. Betty," I said as I walked in with a smile, pretending not to smell the overwhelming stench in her room. I wanted to cover my nose, but I couldn't. It would have been impolite. Betty didn't acknowledge my entrance. She just laid on her bed, face-up. Her physical appearance made me wonder how long she must have been in that position!

"How are you feeling this morning Ms. Betty?" I said. Still, she didn't answer; instead, her body remained motionless with her eyes riveted to the ceiling.

"Are you alright?" I added. Without saying a word, she waved her right hand at me, signaling she had heard me, but wasn't in the mood for useless chitchat. I wasn't disturbed by her demeanor because it was her nature.

Betty knew she had a doctor's appointment that morning and this is what made her act as stubborn as a mule. She didn't want to leave the 'comfort' of her bed because she hated going to Doctors North. Who wouldn't? Her medical examination that morning was very invasive. Joyce was concerned Betty may have contracted an infection which was causing her to experience constant pain in the area where her feet had been amputated. For her own wellbeing, it was imperative she saw her doctor to get to the root cause of her inflammation. Poor woman, tragedy befell her when her path crossed a drunk driver.

"Ms. Betty!" I called her name again, alerting her of my closeness to her bed. She continued to ignore me. It wasn't personal. As I drew close, I put on my latex gloves, ready to detangle her from her sheets. Undisturbed, Betty continued gazing up to the ceiling.

"I would like to help you get ready for your doctor's visit, Ms. Betty!" I said. She remained silent and motionless as though I wasn't even there. I bent over her body and reached for her blanket. 'Oh! What a foul smell. What a funky foul smell!' I thought. The stench was so overpowering I felt like bolting out of the room. Betty remained stock-still and hardly spoke a word as though her lips were sealed. I stuck both my hands underneath the blanket and struggled to roll her body towards mine. She didn't bulge. She was as heavy as a rock. Inwardly, I thought she may have been pressing her body deeper into her bed to make it harder for me to move her. It took several times of tugging that her body bulged slightly toward me. I wanted to prop her comfortably so as to swerve her sideways into her wheelchair and then help her out of bed and to the bathroom. She was no help. She flopped back onto her back like a fish at sea. Stock-still, she laid there, in that wet bed, face-up. Because her body was like dead weight, my efforts to move her were useless. She was dazed in such an unnerving way that a bad thought flashed my mind. What if she had a stroke and can't talk? Immediately, I panicked, unsure of what to do. Her eyes remained open like an entrance to a tunnel and had zeroed in on the ceiling. I paused as my eyes followed hers hoping to see what it was she found so fascinating. There was nothing save for the whiteness of the ceiling. I was moved to pity by just looking at her, forgetting the putrid smell of her body. Filled with sorrow, I wondered what she was thinking about or what her life must have been before her accident.

Meanwhile, I could hear commotion outside Betty's door as staff and clients alike went on about their business. I was jolted back to my reality when Betty coughed. I shifted my gaze from the ceiling back to her motionless body.

"Are you okay Ms. Betty?" I said. Still she didn't answer. This unnerved me even more. Aware I had to make haste lest Joyce yell at me, I pushed my hands underneath her sheets again braving the task of rolling her out of bed once and for all. If I didn't succeed, I had no choice, but to seek help, for time was of the essence. 'If she could only assist me a little, which she always did, or turn her body towards me, it would ease my burden,' I thought. I had no such luck. I tugged at her again, but Betty didn't move a muscle. Her body remained as heavy as lead. After trying several times and having failed miserably, I begged her compliance. She obstinately refused to barge. What an enigma! Defeated, I pressed the buzzer for help.

Nobody showed-up on my first buzz as I watched my time dwindle steadily. I pressed the buzzer again. Still, no one came. Panicking, I tried one final time to roll her out of her bed. It was useless. Once more, I pressed the buzzer. Only then did I hear familiar hurried footsteps advancing my way. It wasn't none other than Joyce. By the time she got to Betty's door, she was panting as though she had just completed a marathon.

"What is the *matter* Mary," she said harshly.

Startled by the roughness of her voice, I said meekly, afraid of being reprimanded, "I need help to get Betty out of her bed. She seems to be in a bad mood this morning."

"Is that right Ms. Betty," Joyce said. Her voice was soft and soothing. Betty didn't respond to her either. Her glossy eyes were still looking to the ceiling and she didn't twitch a muscle. Leaning forward towards her, Joyce moved her right hand, making as though she was about to touch her, only to stop midway, expecting Betty to jerk her body, or stop her on the way, but she never did.

She reached out for a pair of hospital gloves which never left Betty's nightstand. She slipped her hands inside, one at a time. White dust flew off the gloves as they snapped tightly around her hands and fingers. Then, she pushed her left hand behind Betty's upper shoulders and the right hand to her bottom.

In a commanding voice, Joyce said, "Let us do it Mary!" I leaned in, pushed my right hand behind Betty's back, and firmly pressed my left hand under her bottom, the opposite of what Joyce had done.

"On a count of one to three, let's do it!" Joyce said.

"One . . . two . . . three!" I said.

"Now!" she said.

In one synchronized haul, we lifted Betty out of her bed onto her wheelchair, blanket and all. A bad stench ambushed us. There was nothing we could do to minimize the smell. We inhaled this odor in stride. What and overpowering and nauseating stench! I almost threw-up. Once Betty was securely seated in her wheelchair, I took a quick glance at her bed. I noticed it was completely soiled. Damn it! No wonder Betty was in such a foul mood. I, too, would have been in a bad mood. I had to change everything on her bed . . . . mattress cover, sheets and pillow cases, blankets. I hadn't anticipated this complication when I began my shift that morning. Suddenly, I was angered at the nightshift girls for leaving Betty in such a mess. It wasn't too much to ask to put a client on a bed pan to avoid this kind of situation. I am sure Betty must have buzzed for help to go to the bathroom. She always did and without fail. The girl who was responsible for this inhumanity was fired that very day. Her action was unpardonable.

There was no shortcut now. Betty's incident doubled my work. Her refusal to do anything doubled my work. Thank goodness Joyce volunteered to give me a helping hand to lessen my burden.

"Mary, why don't you take care of Betty's room and bed while I give her a bath!" she said.

"Thanks a million! You are an angel," I said to her appreciatively, wheeling Betty to the bathroom. Behind me, Joyce followed along.

We untangled Betty from her covers and threw them to the floor, but careful enough not to soil the floor. That would add an additional fifteen minutes of cleaning which I didn't have. We shifted her from the wheelchair to the bathroom seat. I rolled all her soiled beddings and left with them as Joyce turned on the water tap to begin bathing Betty. I heard her adjust the temperature, but I didn't hang on. I walked back to Betty's room only to realize everything was a mess. I looked at my watch and it read seven thirty. I still had to make Betty's bed and clean her room as quickly as I could so as to get to my other clients. They all had to be ready for their breakfast and at the dining table no later than eight thirty . . . What a challenge! Damn it! I had to hassle now. Quickly, I got clean sheets and blankets, changed the linen on Betty's bed, picked clean clothes for her and tidied everything before leaving. It took about fifteen minutes. Before leaving, I grabbed the soiled beddings and dropped them off into the laundry bin.

I dashed to Cherry Dorson's room next. What a contrast it was from Betty's room. It was so clean and freshly scented with vanilla.

Cherry was a much older woman than Betty, but looking at her, you couldn't tell. Although her hair had grayed, her white skin was tight, but delicate. It didn't sag on her frail frame like most elderly women, but had a glare to it as though she was still in the prime of her youth. She was a little over ninety years old, almost twice my mother. The frame of her body was long, clean, and symmetrical. She was a delight to be around, a sweet jolly old lady. A contrast to Betty. Remotely, she reminded me very much of Grandma Tufroza, only that Grandma was very strong and much older than her, hardened by her impoverishment. Cherry hardly needed assistance. She was a very independent woman. The only kind of aid she required every so often was an occasional reminder of what to do.

Cherry's story was a sad one. She came to St. Grace after the passing of her husband of fifty years. Her children had moved her there because they didn't want her to distract their busy lives. Since her arrival at the center, approximately three years, she never complained about anything. Her two children—a boy and girl—hardly came to see her. The only time they came was on her birthday, which they did as a chore rather than a show of affection. She never showed any bitterness of being abandoned by her children. She was always happy to see them whenever they visited her and happy to see them leave. Her son was more caring than her daughter who lived in California. She once told me she lived with her son, but his wife didn't want her to stay with them anymore. Her daughter-in-law claimed it was too much work to her have live with them. They moved her to St. Grace solely for that reason.

Cherry, too, had her flaws. She was an old toothless woman who couldn't eat any solid food, but not for lack of trying or asking for it. Any food she ate had to be pureed. The most peculiar thing about her was that she couldn't eat unless her brown stuffed bear was fed first. Need I say more? The *oddness* of feeding a stuffed animal made me chuckle every time she asked me to and without fail. To ease the burden of feeding her, I devised a lie. If lying was a sin, I sinned many times during my employment at St. Grace! I deceived an elderly woman and rightfully so! I knew Mama Joy wouldn't have approved, but it was a small *white* lie for Cherry's sake, saving her from starvation. To minimize her feats of anger, all I had to say was, "Ms. Cherry!" I would pause to check her mood. "May I have your bear so I can feed her first before we go to eat?" Cherry would smile back, hand me her bear, and then I would withdraw from her room only to return moments later with its wet nose. Handing her the bear back, she would reach out for it with delight as her pale-white face lit up jovially. She would move her right hand onto the bear's head; much like a child does when petting a favorite pet, letting her hand slowly glide down the bear's neck. She would kiss it on its furry head, and then hand it back to me. Only then would she go through her rituals, whatever those were. If it were in the morning, and I did work mostly morning hours, she brushed her teeth, towel cleaned her face, applied lotion on her alligator skin, and got dressed while I made her bed. After which, I walked her to the dining room where her pureed breakfast awaited her arrival. What a relief! She ate . . . No, she drank her food. If I chanced to work afternoons—the 3:00-11:00 p.m.—shift, I still fed her bear before supper.

That morning, Cherry's mood was no different than other days. I took fifteen minutes to get her ready. I hassled through all my other clients—Bill, Sam, and Jerry. These three were a breeze.

There was nothing complicated with them because they were very independent. I only double checked their space for cleanliness and to ascertain they had completed their morning hygiene.

I finished my morning routine about 10:00 a.m. By then, Joyce had already left with Betty for her appointment and I had a fifteen-minute break. Peaceful moments. I savored this time—every second of it—before I had to worry about lunch. It was only then I remembered my coffee, my sweet coffee. As I walked back to the office to reclaim it, I knew it was not only cold, but also stale. I took the mug, walked to the kitchen, and dumped its contents into the sink. I didn't feel like brewing a new pot even if I had time to do so.

I walked back to the office and sat down for a moment's rest. While there, I couldn't help but feel sorry for most of the clients at St. Grace, like Cherry, some of whom I felt had been abandoned there by their families. Some never even received a visitor all year long. I wondered if some of them could have been better served had they been living with their families. What would Mama Joy say about this arrangement? When break time ended, I resumed work again. It was smooth sailing until lunch time.

On my lunch break, I decided to go out for some fresh air. It was a beautiful afternoon. The sun shone brilliantly above the azure sky and the signs of spring were everywhere. Sprouting tulip bulbs and daffodils, planted in front of St. Grace in late October, had peeked above ground. A red cardinal was perched on a weeping willow near my Diamond. Just what I needed to clear my mind—too much to think about, rent, food, and school. I made my way to my white Civic, hopped inside, and cranked the engine. Road tranced, I headed north on Cleveland Avenue and then west on Dublin Granville looking for the nearest gas station, hardly listening to my favorite Morning Edition Program as it blared on my NPR radio station. My mind was set on the lottery and nothing else. As I drove on, my heart pounded wildly against my ribs like turbulent tidal waves against the ocean shore. Being a non-believer, I still prayed for prudence's sake, hoping for Divine intervention for a win. Images on Dublin-Granville road were the familiar sights— Dunkin Donuts. Hunan House. Huntington Bank. Taco Bell. They appeared and flew before my view as my Michelin tires glided smoothly along the paved road until I came to my favorite gas station. Killing the engine, I pulled into the enthralled gaze of a Speedway attendant.

In my purse, a five dollar bill was securely pinned against the synthetic perforated pockets of my wallet. As I stood there, before the attendant, I knew exactly what I was about to do, revert to the poison of my addiction, the very reason my life was in turmoil. I was certain I had to gamble again, hoping to save face against Sam Snackwell's ultimatum and threats of eviction. Yes! I knew exactly how: First business first, I bet two dollar bills on my license plate number 012. Next, I tabulate my winnings. If I played my numbers straight, I was likely to win at least five hundred dollars, though the odds of my winning were as remote as snow falling on the equator. If I boxed the numbers, I maximized my odds of winning— approximately eighty-three dollars, hardly enough to make a dent in my owed rent. I placed my other bet on my address. I was convinced a straight play would earn me at least five thousand dollars and that was some good change. I felt giddy inside just thinking about it. I still had a dollar left so I purchased a can of

Pepsi and swiftly I walked out of the gas station, into the car, my Diamond. Cruising at thirty-five miles per hour, I headed back to work feeling at ease, convinced I was more likely than not to strike it rich. Once I returned to work, the rest of my day was uneventful.

14

The sun was perfectly balanced on the horizon's dark rim when I returned home nervous about my evening. No sooner had I walked into my apartment than almost immediately I heard the sound of my doorbell—ding-dong. Startled, I tensed-up, afraid to open lest it be Sam Snackwell coming to collect his rent. I heard another ding-dong! This time, it was followed by a gentle tap against the wooden door, emitting soft thumping sounds and demanding my action. This was unlike the way Sam had burst into my apartment the previous day. When the third ding-dong sounded, it was followed by Charlie's gruff voice, "Mary, open the door please, it is me, Charlie. I know you are in there."

"Just a minute Charlie," I said, relieved it wasn't Sam.

"Who the hell did you think I was, Jack the Ripper?" he said, bursting into laughter.

"You might as well have been!" I said behind the door, making ready to click its metallic latch. It moved out of place with ease. I pulled the door towards me as it screeched annoyingly. I gritted my teeth in disgust.

"Sam better oil the hinges of this door before this creaking sound makes me go mad," I said.

"Na' so!" Charlie said in pidgin.

As the door flew open, it brought the outside inside, an intense warm air. There, right before me, stood Charlie dressed in a white T-shirt with the American flag smacked at its center. Above the flag, there was an inscription in a bold red color that read: IF THIS FLAG OFFENDS YOU, I HELP YOU PACK! Charlie looked much disheveled. His eyes were red-hot as though he hadn't slept in days. He was so inebriated I could smell alcohol fumes on his breath.

"May I come in?" he said, squeezing past me and not waiting to be invited in. He nearly knocked me over! His feet wobbled as he struggled to maintain his balance.

"Be my guest," I said, puzzled and with laughter in my eyes.

With his back to me, I saw a sinister-looking black bald eagle plastered at the back of his t-shirt staring at me with menacing eyes. Its head was white-feathered and seemed as though it was about to fly out of his t-shirt and pounce onto me. Its golden pointed beak and pale-yellow eyes were enough to instill fright in me. This was the first time I had ever seen Charlie wearing a patriotic t-shirt.

As he forced his way past me, I became fully aware of how drunk Charlie was. There was no question about this truth. His drunken stupor wasn't out of character, but the way he forced his way into my apartment made me wonder what was eating at him. Immediately, I knew all was not well.

"There is *something* . . . I . . . I . . . neeed to . . . to tell you," he said, slurring his speech and breaking into a cold sweat. He found his way to my couch on which he slumped his body.

"What is up Charlie?" I said, unsure of what else to tell my drunk pal.

"Not much . . . Not much!" he responded dispassionately. I was not convinced. "Really!" he added, seeing my bewildered eyes.

"You could have fooled me!" I said.

"Really . . . I mean it!" he added. "Besides work and work, nothing could be wrong."

"What was it you wanted to tell me then?"

"Mary! Mary! Mary!" he said categorically. "I have been hanging around you far too long. You seem to know me fairly well. I couldn't fool you one bit."

"Uuh" I grunted.

"Okay, you got me," he said. "If I say I am alright, I would be lying to you."

"I know!" I said. On second thought, I added, "Charlie, tell me exactly why you are here!" my tone was icy.

"My sister –oo—oo! I am ready to settle down . . . Really! Me Charlie Crabtree," he said trying to convince me of this colossal decision. No! I believe he was trying to convince himself more than me. "I do! That is what I wanted to tell you!"

"You had to get drunk to come and tell me this?"

"Eeh! Eeh! My sister oo-oo! You know me. I like my beer."

How so true! Charlie once told me that when his mother was pregnant with him, she used to drink Guinness beer every day, claiming her doctor told her it was good for her and the baby. I couldn't tell if that was why he was a borderline alcoholic.

Surprised by the news, reels of Charlie's past life flashed my mind—from those days at DJ Prophets to the present. I didn't see anyone. No. There was no woman in that past. Only once did a woman come to visit him from his country of origin. Charlie claimed his mother was behind the young woman's visit. Unfortunately, a relationship between him and the girl was never meant to be. Papa Dan—his friend of many years—'swept' her off her feet, leaving Charlie in a fit of rage. Nothing of significance happened between Papa and the woman to speak of. If ever there was something special between them, it might have been a one night's fling, and nothing more. Beyond this, the closest Charlie came to having a girlfriend was when he quizzed ladies with his stupid spelling test: "How do you spell milk? What do cows drink?" It all ended there, in some crappy nightclub, not in his bedroom. Yet, here was Charlie proclaiming his desire for marriage.

"You got someone in mind?" I said, even though I knew what his answer would be.

"No, but I have a lot of love to give," he said. His mind seemed to be a tasseled squall with wild dreams.

Unamused with his thinking, I hoped Charlie wasn't cracking-up like Kobie had months ago. Besides, his life was as fragmented as Kobie's had been. We all were, but there was one difference. Kobie was rotting somewhere in a mental institution. If not, he was probably dead.

"When I find this lady," Charlie noted, "I swear I will shower her with love. I will worship the ground upon which she walks."

There was a slight sparkle in his dull red eyes. The booze seemed to have robbed his eyes of their usual luster.

The strangeness of Charlie's revelation caused me some anxiety. A man his age, in his late forties, was probably experiencing a midlife crisis. Or perhaps his mother was pestering him to settle down. Most African mothers were peculiar that way.

Suddenly, I recalled how my own mother had beleaguered me a couple of years ago. I was twenty-five then and unattached. I was sitting in my living room when my phone rang. Those days, phone calls from home weren't a common occurrence. When I picked up the receiver, I was surprised to hear my mother's voice. After we exchanged the usual pleasantries, she 'popped' the question:

"Upanga!" she said. She let a moment of silence elapse. for a second, wondered if the line had disconnected. "Have you ever given any thought about settling down?" Before I could answer, she added, "When are you ever going to finally settle down?"

"I don't know Mama!" I said, startled by her questioning. It was the most honest answer I could have given her at the time, but that was a lie. I had no intentions of getting married. I truly believed marriage was overrated, but I couldn't tell her that lest I break her heart. Another time, Father called me only to ask me the same thing Mama had asked previously. 'Upanga! . . . Your mother asked me to call you so I could ask you something." He sounded very sincere.

I wasn't thinking of my prior conversation with Mama about marriage.

"Okay," I said. "Is Mama alright?"

"Yes, she is fine."

"Does she need anything?" I said.

"It's not what she needs," he said. "She wants to know when you are planning to get married."

I gave him the same response I had given Mama. He didn't pressure me about it and I didn't elaborate on my answer.

Months after our conversation, when I visited home, Mama Joy would later tell me it was Father who had asked her to call me, talk to me, and ask me about my future marriage plans.

I was reeled back to my pulsing present when Charlie coughed.

"Are you feeling alright Charlie?" I said.

"Oh, I couldn't be better. Believe me! When I find her, she will fall madly in love with me. Me . . . Charlie Crabtree . . . mark my words!"

"What if you meet this woman, and she doesn't love you back?"

"Believe me, I beg! . . . She wouldn't have a choice. I wouldn't give her an excuse not to fall in love with me. I can even imagine her heart racing at the mention of my name. I can just see her tossing in her bed yearning for me, her mind swirling with unquenched passion."

"Charlie, dream on!" I said, and dreaming he was. There was no way, given his current situation, he could find love . . . not unless he changed his ways. All he ever did was work and booze. Booze had gotten him in more trouble than he dared to admit. He had lost his driver's license because of it, driving under the influence. To this day, more than thirty years have come and gone, but Charlie doesn't own a car or have a driver's license. That's not all. Charlie doesn't even have a bank account. What a shame!

"I will be the most honest man she has ever met."

"What if she is not honest with you?"

"Come off of it! I beg . . . Believe me my Sister! Eeh! Heee . . . . she will. I will smother her with love, true love. She won't even know what hit her," he said boisterously.

"Charlie, there are no guarantees in love, not even in life."

"You don't know what you are talking about! It is me . . . Charlie we are talking about."

"How can you be so conceited like that?"

"Because I know myself! No one can toot my praises better than me.

"I give up!"

"My darling sister I tell you, the woman of my dreams will have no *choice*," he said emphasizing the word *choice*.

"Don't darling me Charlie," I said playfully.

"Darling! Darling! Darling!" he paused, checking to see if I was offended. "You are one of my dearest friends. That is why I am telling you these things."

"Who is the other person?"

"Eeh! Eeh! Is that even a question to ask? My Mother, of course!" And that couldn't have been far from the truth. Save for distance, Charlie's relationship with his mother was solid gold. He always said they were kindred spirits.

"Alright then! When you find this person . . . that is, if you haven't found her already, shower her with all the endearing darlings you can."

"I guess I have to work on that."

"Good luck Charlie . . . I mean it."

"Thanks, but I don't need luck," he said making ready to go back to his apartment.

"You take care of yourself and stop all this foolishness about getting married to a mysterious woman . . . stop building castles in the air!" I said as Charlie walked out of my living room into the womb of the universe. I, too, stood up and walked behind him to the door.

"Later Mary," he said.

I watched him as he walked to his apartment.

'What a restless soul under the remote stars of sky! What a character!' I thought.

I saw him unlock his door, open it, and then vanish behind it.

The sun had completely vanished from the western sky when Charlie left my apartment. Its once orange-purple glossed glare had been transformed into a vast expanse of blackness, save for the dotted flicker of city lights. I latched my door out of fear of being ambushed by Sam again. A repeat of yesterday was a definite 'No!' I had learned my lesson from his previous intrusion into my apartment the other day. After he left, I had made a solemn promise to myself there and then to lock it at all the times. No matter what!

I walked back to my couch and sat down in total darkness, not bothering to turn on my lights or television. A vulgar mood of loneliness ambushed me. Alone in a cold world without pity, alone in a foreign land without any one close of kin, away from my family, away from everything that defined me. Weary and tired, I sat there, watching time march on at a steady pace. In my silence, two things nagged me. Thing one. Why Charlie had, all of a sudden, been struck by a desire to marry. At age forty-five, he, a senior bachelor, masqueraded as a womanizer. How could he give up all that for marriage? Whatever prompted his yearning to marry, I'll never know. Perhaps he realized prancing around with women and incessantly drinking alcohol was a detriment to his wellbeing.

Thing two. I was belabored by my life's hardships to a point of paralysis. I recalled the day when everything forever changed in my life. It was one Monday night in 1995, when I received a call from my sister Liz at 2:00 a.m. Liz never called me, but hearing the trembling quiver in her voice when she said 'Hello" and her labored breathing, I knew all was not well. She didn't have to tell me. I could feel it thousands of miles away. When she announced: 'Anna is dead!' I was grief stricken and smothered by the night's darkness. Her unexpected passing left a big void in my heart. She was two years younger than me. I never went to her funeral because I had no money for a ticket. I also knew my visa was about to expire and

I couldn't risk the trip. Mama would later tell me she was poisoned to death when I returned home to pay my last respects. Before then, I had conjured-up many different scenarios of how it all happened. One which seemed more plausible was that her mother in-law had found her stone-cold, with her body firmly pressed in an armchair under the canopy of a gum tree. It was as though she was asleep, but she had already expired. She tried to wake her up, but no shaking could reel her back to the land of the living. She was not sick prior to her demise. She had simply propped her head on the back of her armchair after her afternoon meal, closed her eyes as though she was taking her siesta, never to reopen them again. Another rumor had it that she had been struck by the belligerent eyes of the evil-eyed woman. Her mother in-law must have missed all the signs of death she had noticed. She had dismissed them as meaningless: Like the sinister hooting of an owl, a creature she could not chase out of her compound regardless of how many times she had tried. Even a hot burning splinter thrown at the ominous bird could not purge her home of its evilness. Then, there was the sudden loss of two of her calves that had occurred without any warning or sign of illness, heralding an eminent death. There was also the sudden chicken flu which claimed all her birds. This was the final sign, but she missed *it* . . . death. She felt *it* all around her, but knew *it* not. When *it* wagged *its* head annoyingly in her home, when the sting of death unleashed its venom on her family, she understood everything.

This was hardly what happened to Anna. Rumor had it that her mother in-law had poisoned her following the birth of her third child, a boy. That was the honest truth my mother revealed to me when I went to pay her my final respects a year later. When we visited her home, my parents and I never found her grave. They had buried her on a farmland, which they had later ploughed and to which they had grown beans and maize. We tussled with bean vines and a maze of maize unable to locate her grave. There was no identifying marker placed where she had been laid to rest. She was lost to all of us as though she never was. I left her home distraught and forever altered by her end, having realized the folly in people's heart—or our humanity—that we, as mortals, have the power of choosing good or evil deeds. For both reside in us and one cannot exist without the other. Oftentimes, evil overpowers goodness, just as it had overpowered Anna's mother in-law.

I must have fallen asleep to my thoughts of my younger sister Anna. I woke up a couple of hours later to a roiling stomach. I was so hungry I could have eaten just about anything. Unfortunately, I didn't have any food in my pantry to speak of. I couldn't even go to McDonalds to buy a hamburger. I only had fifty cents to my name, the change I had received after buying a can of Pepsi earlier on in the day at Speedway gas station. I considered rummaging through my purse and everywhere else in my apartment for loose change, hoping to get enough to buy a value meal from Wendy's.

This idea inspired me greatly. Determined to tame my hunger, I rose from my couch and headed straight for the refrigerator. I opened it, but it was as empty as a bird's nest. There was no milk. There was no juice. There was no bread. There were no eggs. There was nothing save for a container of plain rice I had cooked about a week ago. I picked the container and looked inside. A greenish hue had begun to form around the edges of the container and the rice, and it smelled awful. I couldn't eat it even if I were starving. A dog couldn't eat it. And even if it hadn't started to mold, there was no beef or chicken stew with which to serve it. I dumped the rice in the trash, washed the container, and then I began to ransack through everything I could put my hands on looking for coins— The kitchen drawers. The counter top. I looked inside my coin jar where, once in a while, I had the tendency to drop my coins. It, too, was empty. The bathroom cabinets followed. I left nothing unturned. I saw nothing. No. I found nothing. I must have emptied everything awhile back. The exact day or hour I undertook such action evaded me. I walked to my coat closet and inspected my coat pockets. There was nothing in them either. Feeling distraught and deflated, I said, 'Where is Mama Joy when I need her?' Had she been with me, I would have asked her for maize the way Grandma Tufroza did whenever she visited our home.

I took my search to the bedroom. The dresser was the most logical place to begin. I pulled out the first drawer and ransacked it. Still, there was nothing. I checked in all the three drawers and they, too, were empty. 'Oof!' I let out a despairing sigh. 'What to do! What to do,' I thought. Suddenly, I remembered I hadn't looked in my slacks. Feeling as though I had attained renewed energy, I reached out for my first pair. I ran my right hand inside the pockets. They felt soft and cold, as cold as ice. Nothing was inside except a few strands of thread that got stuck to my nails. I tossed it aside and pulled out another one. As I checked its pockets, my fingers felt something. My heart skipped a beat. 'This must be my lucky day,' I thought. Gingerly, I pulled it out, my heart pounding with excitement. When I saw what it was, my heart sank with disappointment. It was a week old receipt from Midstate Educator's Credit Union with my account balance of $19. I crushed the receipt and tossed it into the trash bin like all useless things and where it belonged. I checked in a third and fourth pair of slacks. They, too, were empty. Two more pants to go. Both were jeans— one blue and the other black—which I seldom wore. I didn't think I had anything in them, but checked them nonetheless. Before deciding on which one to empty its pockets first, I reverted to a nonsensical childhood game I played every so often whenever I was uncertain of what I wanted to choose:

Kuruguse
Mee
Kuruguse
Mee
Umweeri gula duuda
Gula duuda likalikali jamba
Jamba jamba teletele lumbwa

My hand landed on the black one. 'Good!' Black was my lucky charm color. I thrust my right hand deep into its back pocket. There was nothing, not even a piece of paper. '*Wow! Some bad luck?*' I said almost giving-up hope. Before I tossed this one away, there was only one pocket left, which I had not checked. I pushed my hand inside, expecting the expected, nothing. To my surprise, my fingers touched something cold and papery. I desperately wanted to pull it out that instant, but I refrained. What it if it was another bank receipt? What would I do then? These thoughts flashed my mind for a second. And without realizing it, I was holding an old green paper in my hand. It was a five dollar bill.

One could have seen my excitement! I immediately dropped on my knees, looked up to my ceiling, saying 'Thank God it is you Abe

Lincoln.' Elated I kissed the crumbled bill aware my food trouble for that day was over.

Without wasting time, I grabbed my car keys and purse, and hurriedly left the apartment. I thought of going to McDonalds for a cheeseburger, but going to Kroger made more sense. I sped down E. Dublin Granville road, driving fifty miles per hour in a forty-five speed zone. As I did so, I hoped no policeman was in the vicinity. Luck was on my side this time. I made my way to the store in a matter of minutes. The store was jam packed with shoppers. I went straight to the meat department. I grabbed a packet of ground beef, which was much cheaper. I marched to the pasta aisle where I settled for a box of Italy's number one Barilla Pasta: Rigatoni, "Al Dente." The direction on the box read: "Perfection in thirteen to fifteen minutes." Good. I added-up my total for both items (meat and the pasta). It came to three dollars. Super! I still had two more dollars and fifty cents, just enough to buy a small Sunny Delight drink and a head of broccoli. Both were on sale for a combined one dollar and twenty-five cents. In a matter of minutes, I was standing to the gripped gaze of a Kroger clerk.

"Do you have your Kroger Plus Card Miss?"

"Of course," I said. I reached into my purse and pulled out my card. I handed it to the cashier, who took it without saying a word and swiped it. She handed it back to me.

"Your total is $5.26!" I handed her my crumpled five dollar bill and my two quarters. She punched several keys on her cash register, as its metallic latch flew open. She quickly and steadily dropped the money in the five dollar slot and the coins in its proper place. "Your change is twenty-four cents," she said handing me the money.

"Thanks," I said, moving steadily away from her as I headed for the exit door.

Once in my car, I sped back home, but again afraid of the police. I also hoped Sam Snackwell wouldn't be at my door awaiting my return determined to execute his ultimatum. Thank goodness when I arrived at home, there was no sign of Sam Snackwell. Besides, it was late for him to make his showing. I went straight to the kitchen and prepared my meal . . . a complete meal. What a delight it was!

After my dinner, I turned off all my lights, collapsed on my couch, and wrapped my body in my comforter. I closed my eyes contented I still had a place to call home. Perhaps, Sam had given me a day's reprieve. I closed my eyes to the world, to all the Sam Snackwells of the world, to everything . . .

15

The next day I returned home from work before dusk. The winter months had long come and gone, paving way for an early spring. This was true to Jym Ganahl's, a meteorologist, pronounced prediction that morning, "We're out of the woods folks! Spring is now upon us." His words, which were still fresh on my mind, had a good ring to my ears. Given my disdain for the winter season, I welcomed the prospect of an early spring. The temperature had risen exponentially from the low thirties and had come close to seventy degrees. What a beautiful evening! The sun was now low to the west and most people were out enjoying a nice warm spring breeze. Others loitered about aimlessly. A neighbor's two sons were playing chase around the complex. Several girls were riding their bicycles in stride. The air split with jolly voices of happy folks. I took in all these sights with a smile before walking to my apartment.

Because I had had a rough day at work, I didn't want to think about anything whatsoever! I was ready to embrace the comfort of my small flat. As I walked inside, I locked the door behind me and dropped everything I had on the floor. Then, I dropped my body on my couch like a log. This was nothing new. Only then did I, for once, experience the throbbing pains in my legs. I reclined on the couch and closed my eyes. I didn't think about turning on my television. I must have fallen asleep because I awoke to the sound of a ringing telephone. I didn't have my watch on, but I surmised it was about 9:00 p.m. My living room was already engulfed in blackness. An unnerving darkness too eerie to escape the mind. I moved my eyes to the phone and then looked outside, through the cracks in my blinds. The outside, too, was pitch black. The intrusive ringing of my phone sounded again. I moved my eyes away from the outside to the phone, debating whether to answer or ignore it. I chose the former.

I reached for the receiver and said, "Hello!"

"Hello my Sister. It's me . . . Charlie," came the voice on the other end of the line.

"Oh my goodness Charlie! Why are you calling me so late?" I said irritated.

"Aah! I beg . . . it's not that late," he said.

"Not to you!" I said.

"I am sorry to have intruded on your sleep. I wouldn't have called this late if it wasn't important."

"It better be!"

"Na' so . . . Na' so!" he said, forgetting I didn't speak pidgin. "You cannot believe what happened to me today!" There was a quiver in his voice. It was a familiar quiver. Much like the quiver I had heard in my sister's voice when she announced to me the news about Anna's death.

'Oh! Brother not again,' I mumbled under my breath. Charlie's stories were always tangled tall tales.

"Can't this wait until tomorrow," I said groggily.

"No!"

"It better be good!" I said again.

"You can't believe what happened today!" he said once more, sounding like a broken record.

"Believe what Charlie!" I said harshly, untangling myself from my comforter. From the sound of his voice, I sensed something was terribly wrong.

"Papa is dead!" he said in a trembling voice.

"What?" I said in disbelief, startled and stupefied by a truth so painful to fathom.

"Yeah! Papa is dead," he said again, as though I had not heard him the first time.

Suddenly, I felt bad and foolish for the way I had reacted.

Papa was Charlie's best friend of many years. They were kindred spirits and inseparable. Their friendship didn't end when Papa allegedly 'stole' his woman a few years back. Charlie believed a woman belonged to a man only when they were in bed together. Other times, she belonged to the world. If she the woman in question had been his, she wouldn't have sought another man. That was why he forgave Papa for his betrayal, claiming had she been his, she would have remained faithful to him.

The two met years ago as students at a local Community College, but there was one significant difference between them. Papa finished his associate degree and joined a local university in Ohio where he completed both his undergraduate and master's degrees in Political Science. Charlie never finished any academic degree. He lost his way in the process. He met a white girl, fell madly in love with her, but she dumped him and broke his heart. He never recovered from his broken heart.

Papa was a middle-aged man from Kenya, skinny as they get, with a kind and fatherly spirit. We all nicknamed him Papa for these reasons. He was the first Kenyan man I knew with jerry curls. He reminded me of the character Darrel, in Eddie Murphy's classic movie, *Coming to America,* and was very proud of it. I called him 'greasy head' because the stuff he put on his hair always made it look too oily, and whenever he sat somewhere and rested his head on something, he left a giant blotch of grease. He even had a moustache like Darrel. Not many people knew his *real* name— Jonas Oduor. Those who knew it never called him by it. They simply called him Papa. We *all* called him Papa. Every weekend, he would invite us to his house, cook, and buy us drinks. He and Charlie liked beer very much, but he never finished a bottle. Because he was a workhorse, he was tired a lot. Whenever we went to his house, we always found food ready. There would be loud Congolese music—Diblo Dibala, Zaiko Langa Langa, or Pepe Kale—playing in the background. After serving us drinks, he would take his own, but always fell asleep on the couch with it in hand after only a few sips amid a ruckus of loud jolly folks eating, listening to music, and making merry. Strange enough, he never spilt his drink, even if we heard him snoring. Once I tried to pull a can out of his hand, but he woke up, rearranged himself in his couch, took a sip of his beer, closed his eyes and, within no time, he started snoring again as though nothing had happened. His snoring was always as loud as a pig's grunt.

"What happened? Was he sick?" I said, tossing my comforter to the floor alerted by the tragic news.

"Well, not exactly!"

"What do you mean?"

"The police came to question me at work earlier on today."

"The *police?*"

"Yes! They questioned me about his death."

"You didn't kill him . . . did you?"

"No, stupid! They said he bled to death."

"Bled to death?" I said in disbelief. "How did that happen? Did someone stab him? Was there a scuffle?" I questioned Charlie randomly, hardly giving him time to respond.

"No. . . I am not sure. They said he committed suicide. He jumped out of his upstairs bedroom, landing on the hard asphalt of their parking lot. The glass from his bedroom window must have cut him. . . Nobody was around to help him. The police are ruling his death a suicide."

"Oh Dear!"

"There was no sign of forced entry into his apartment . . . Nothing, and I mean, nothing was disturbed. His door was bolted from inside. There is no way anyone could have been in the house with him when he jumped."

"I am speechless! Dumbfounded!" I said. "How could this have happened to one of us?" I wondered out loud, not expecting a response from Charlie. A meaningful silence followed, allowing me to absorb the shock of a life ended in tragedy, a fragmented life. Neither here nor there.

"Someone found his body sprawled in a pool of blood in the parking lot two doors away from his apartment. He crawled several inches from where he fell, leaving behind a trail of blood," Charlie continued. Then, unexpectedly, he broke into a rant. "My sister oo-oo! My sister oo-oo! I should have seen it. I should have seen it coming my Sister!"

"Seen what? Papa's so called *suicide*?"

"Yes! I should have seen it."

Puzzled, I wondered what it was he had inadvertently omitted in his story about Papa's tragic passing. Could it have been prevented? Can suicide be prevented? What if he didn't want to be saved?

"Charlie," I said calmly, though I could feel tears stinging the rims of my eyelids. "Why don't you take a deep breath and then tell me everything you know that happened . . . from start to finish. Right now, you are not making any sense to me."

"Okay," Charlie said. He roughly cleared his throat. I sat bolt upright, reached out for the switch of my living room light and flickered it on.

"Last night," he said, "I stayed up very late. You know me . . . I like watching my television . . . I was very tired. Mr. Fairland, my boss, had worked me very hard that day." He paused for a second.

Charlie worked for Nu Look Suit Factory where he pressed and loaded packaged goods for shipment. His job was physical. That was why, at the end of the day, he took pleasure in his beer. The factory has long been closed now.

"I was drinking my beer just relaxing and watching my favorite Stephen King based movie, *The Shining,*" Charlie continued. "It was showing on TNT. When the movie ended at eleven, I changed the channel to NBC. The news came on. I drank another beer. Jay Leno's Tonight Show came on. I drank another beer. I began to feel light-headed. It must have been after midnight when I went to bed."

"Charlie! What happened?" I said exasperated, wanting him to skip all the unnecessary details. Charlie didn't seem to be in a hurry to get there.

"My Sister, when my head hit my pillow, I zonked out. Really! . . . I zonked out!"

"Well, then?"

"I must have been asleep for quite a while because when my phone rang, it was probably three or four in the morning. I was startled from my sleeping, thinking it was Mama Miswa, my mother, calling from home. She always calls me in the middle of the night. People at home are so screwed-up about American time. Only it wasn't her, but Papa"

"At 3:00 a.m.?"

"Yes! He didn't sound well at all. No. Whatever he said didn't make any sense to me."

"What did he say? What was wrong with him?"

"I couldn't tell you. All I know is I didn't want to open my eyes out of fear of being unable to fall back asleep," Charlie rumbled on unaware, he, too, was keeping me awake.

"I was tired and groggy—with all the beer I had drank! . . . I yelled at him. Can you believe that! I yelled at him. Papa wasn't irritated by it; instead, he said, 'Charlie, there is something crawling under my bed. It wants to get me.'"

"What?" I said.

"I am not kidding you my sister-oo!" Charlie said. "The *bobo* said that there was something crawling right underneath his bed."

"Are you dreaming Papa?" I asked him.

"No, I am not. Believe me . . . If you don't believe me, come and see it for yourself. There is something underneath my bed," he said sounding distraught.

"You mean like a boogeyman?" I said to him.

"I don't know!" he said. "There is something underneath my bed!" he added emphatically and frantically.

"I couldn't help him at that hour of the night. You know me . . . I don't drive," Charlie said. His tone was full of regret. "I assumed he must have been dreaming. Or maybe he was sleep walking and had called me in his nightmare. You know people do that!" Charlie said trying to convince me of it.

"Begrudgingly, I pried my head off my pillow," he said. "I looked at my alarm clock and it was three thirty in the morning. Rats Papa! I have to be at work at seven in the morning."

Papa didn't listen. He kept on repeating the same thing, "There is something underneath my bed!"

"Papa! Do you know what time it is?"

"No! I don't care about that. There is something underneath my bed," he obstinately insisted.

"Okay man, I believe you," I said convinced that Papa wouldn't let me go back to sleep unless I agreed with him. "Tell you what man, do me a favor!"

"What?"

"You get your bible, read a couple of verses, put the bible underneath your pillow, and go back to sleep."

"Okay," he said replacing the receiver, ending our bizarre conversation as abruptly as it had begun. I don't know if he ever did."

"I, too, replaced mine, closed my eyes once more and went back to sleep, not at all thinking about the strangeness of Papa's phone call. I didn't make a big deal out of it until this morning when the police came to see me at work. I connected the tragedy of his passing right away to the conversation he and I had had the previous night. . . I could have done something to save him, but I didn't"

"What could you have done Charlie?"

"I could have gone to see him in the morning. . . Check on him. You know!" There was silence. I didn't say anything, neither did Charlie.

Finally I said, "Papa probably had a nervous breakdown and you didn't see it! Truly no one could have seen it."

The impersonal lifestyle in American had converted all of us into mindless robots . . . forcing us to disregard our humanity. Papa must have been struck by the abyss of solitude and loneliness, a malady which had smitten Kobie to lunacy. A lost soul. Papa's death, *at his own hand*, was taboo to those from his Luo ethnicity. Culturally, he must have dived to Hades on tongues of fire.

"I should have gone to see him!" Charlie said remorsefully.

"You didn't know he was going to kill himself . . . Stop blaming yourself," I said, trying to console him. "What is done is done. There is nothing you can do now to alter his fate."

"He was my friend!"

"He was my friend too, remember?"

"I know!"

"Do you believe in destiny?"

"What does it have to do with Papa?"

"Well, what is destined to happen, happens no matter our intentions. His time had come. There was nothing you could have done to alter that truth. No one could have saved him, but himself. He had to go even if it were like a poof of dust."

"I could have saved him!" he said melancholically.

"What could you have done differently?"

"As I said, I should have gone to see him in the morning. Only I woke up late and didn't think of it."

"That is why I said may be it was his destiny. Destiny is destiny!"

"You don't understand!"

"Make me!"

"When I returned home from work this evening, I found a frantic message he had left on my answering machine."

"What did it say?"

"'I need help!' That is all: 'I need help!'" Charlie said.

I listened keenly and with curious intensity.

"That was March 9, 2001 at 9:30 a.m. He must have jumped right after that. It was creepy hearing his voice on my machine knowing he was already dead. I wondered why he hadn't called 911. That would have made more sense than him calling me."

I agreed with Charlie on that point. Papa should have dialed 911. He must have not been in the right frame of mind to do so. I, too, would have been spooked to hear a dead man's voice on my answering machine soliciting for help.

"So where is his body now?"

"I don't know, but maybe in the morgue," he said. "They have to perform an autopsy. Watch the 11:00 o'clock news tonight. They might have something on him. Someone told me ABC News reported the incident at 5:30 p.m."

I told Charlie I, too, had seen the report, but I had not connected the nameless individual mentioned to anyone I knew. Such news was not uncommon on our local news briefs. The anchorman simply announced, "*An unidentified black male was found dead in a parking lot on the northeast side of Columbus near Morse road. Police are not sure of the cause of his death. The case is now under investigation.*" That was all there was to it. When I heard the news, all

I remember thinking was: "Poor Fellow! Perhaps it was a drug deal case gone badly." Little did I know the unnamed man would turn out to be Papa! Papa didn't do drugs . . . At least, I didn't know if he ever tried them. He drank beer after work, just like Charlie, and nothing more!

After my conversation with Charlie came to an end, I turned my lights off and sat in silence paralyzed by Papa's passing and absorbing the impact of the news to my life. My heart bled for his mother who would soon receive the chilling call announcing her son's passing just as much as I received mine when my sister Anna died.

When the 11:00 p.m. o'clock news came on, Papa was given three-seconds of fame, a repeat of the 5:30 p.m. o'clock news. The nameless *Blackman* was simply another statistic . . . an automaton lost at sea. I swathed my body in my comforter, set my television on the sleep mode (thirty minutes to be exact), and closed my eyes, as darkness hung upon my heart like a cloak. Although my ears were attuned to the news, I hardly listened. Not even to the weather, the very reason I watched news at night. It didn't matter anymore this time . . .

Papa's tragic passing thrust our small Kenyan immigrant community into an avalanche of tumult. One man was singled out as culprit. All was because of a girl. The man never came to the fundraising and missed his wake altogether. He claimed his car skidded on the road as he made his way to the funeral. A few superstitious souls construed this happenstance as a sure sign of the man's culpability in Papa's death. Tempers flared tempered with speculations, of the very nature of his dying: Schizophrenia, a man gone mad, foul play, suicide, women, or simply, an unfortunate end to a life lived in utter disharmony. When a fundraising event was held, people gave donation after donation. Men and women. Young and old. Some, out of respect for the dead, attended his fundraising event. Some, out of curiosity, wanted to confirm that the man, fondly known as Papa, was indeed dead. All gathered in a room at Truman Hotel off of Busch Boulevard to discuss what ought to be done with his remains: Ship them home to his mother. Or cremate them. Others simply queried: How much would it cost? How much money did he have to his name? Does he have any relatives here? Would the body go home alone? Or would someone have to accompany it? What the hell did it matter anymore? The man was dead. Stone cold.

Like most of us, Papa had come to America chasing a dream, to escape the clutches of poverty of his motherland, believing his education was key to his material success. That dream soon became entangled in a web of racism, alcohol, and women, too tough to untangle. Though he had earned two degrees, a partial dream fulfilled, he hit an unexpected barricade. Out of immigration status, deportation or the jaws of prison became a looming reality. Gravitating towards the unthinkable, he opted for matrimonial bliss in the arms of an American belle, a temporary fix, which moved him farther and farther away from his dream and closer to his eventual demise. He got married. He became a father; it was expected. Three children later, the marriage went sour. Fearing incarceration and deportation, he faced a quagmire, of either abiding by the law or prison. He sacrificed his comfort, slaving in three thankless jobs, just to pay child support for his children he was never allowed to see. Money was never enough and, soon, his body yielded to the stress of life. He lost control over it, becoming merely a broken and fragmented man. He couldn't go back home, for the shame of returning empty handed was greater than his self-imposed enslavement. As his body withered like a leaf, so did his spirit. For a spirit in tumult could not forever languish in despair. To free it from the shackles of living, he made his expeditious exit in a forceful tumble through a gaping hole of shattered glass, down, down, down, and like a ball he slammed onto the hard dry asphalt, staining it red, all in the name of freedom . . .

The afternoon of Papa's wake, the March sky grew dark with massive clouds that hung in high puffs like giant cotton balls. Then the bowels of sky burst open. It began to rain nonstop drenching an already saturated earth. We all braved the weather as we made our way to the wake.

At the funeral home, all Kenyans who knew the man came in droves. Other friends, too, came. Not his children for whom he had given his all. Eulogies were read, acknowledging the man he once was. Some of us offered our eulogies of his contributions to our lives. We were all touched. We all sang our favorite dirges in Kiswahili committing his spirit to God's tender mercies—*Mwamba Wenye Imara*, Rock of Ages; *Chakutumaini Sina*, My Hope is Built on Nothingness; and *Bwana U Sehemu Yangu*, Thou My Everlasting Portion. A non-denominational prayer was offered, even if the man hardly set foot in church. Alone as he had lived and died, alone he had been boxed-up and sent to his mother across the oceans. Though, Papa's untimely demise, like Kobie's nervous breakdown, would soon be understood as a consequence of his alien existence on American soil: Loneliness, loss of identity, misguided goals, unfulfilled dreams, or unfulfilled relationships. All these issues were hallmark to the loss of anchorage in his life, *our* lives, in a country where freedom and material success was highly coveted, but an illusion to us, new African immigrants. Here in the land of the *free* we live fragmented lives . . .

Ultimately, we shipped Papa's unaccompanied remains in a box to Kenya . . . not a fancy casket. Just a brown box like useless cargo. His passport 'pinned' onto the box to identify him. What a shock it was for a mother to receive her son in this manner. We didn't have privy to his funeral back home, but days following his burial, his mother, too, died of a broken heart.

16

One day, a couple of weeks after Papa's remains had been shipped back to his home, I awoke at 6:00 a.m. to a pounding headache. With my body still tucked underneath my blanket, I pried my eyes open and peeked through the cracks in my window. I saw no sign of light. The outside was dark, as dark as my heart. Feeling lethargic, I closed my eyes, again contemplating my life's choice: Why I had left home to chase a dream . . . An insatiable madness which had galvanized my exit and bled my loneliness. Only a couple of young men from my village had been daring enough to take on the challenge, chasing leaping fancies of success in a foreign land. Nothing good came out of their trouble. One of them who had gone to Greece for study returned home empty handed. He took to the bottle and perished in an inferno. The other left and never returned; he vanished into oblivion. When his parents passed on, he never came for their funerals. Then, there was me, doomed to absorb the punishment that followed my permanent uprooting. I was, therefore, completely unable to see how America was that sacred place destined to make me achieve my happiness . . . *real* happiness.

As I laid there, I dreaded going to work, but my impending eviction was justification enough. For it hung around me like a black shroud. I also mulled over why Sam hadn't showed up at my apartment to collect my rent. I speculated he must have had another date with Anheuser Busch Brewery and, like Charlie, he loved his beer.

When I finally rolled out of bed a half an hour later, I swung my legs over the side of my bed and sprang to my feet. The floor felt very cold as the soles of my feet came into contact with it. It was cold enough to drive away the residual effect of sleepiness I still felt. I walked to the window and drew my drapes. The clouds dominated the skyline making the morning have the semblance of gloom, a kind of gloom that comes cloaked in death. Without making my bed, something I hardly did, I raced to the kitchen to start my coffee in my Proctor Silex Coffee Maker, dashed to the bathroom, took a quick shower, and got dressed loathing the thought of going to work.

I returned to the kitchen to find my coffee ready. Hurriedly, I poured some in my mug, added some cold milk and guzzled it, not wanting to be late. I took no pleasure in it as time was not on my side.

When I left home for work, the sky was heavily covered with dark clouds. Sporadic patches of blue made occasional appearance. I paused to take in this sight, while inwardly, I wished my day would be incident free, with Betty being perky for a change and Cherry cheery as always. Both were.

At work, everything was routine and went as expected. I couldn't escape the stale smell of St. Grace. Joyce and everyone else was their usual selves, save for Bill Yeager, my other client. He was a different caliber of a man than all the other folks with whom I worked. His mood fluctuated from happy to sad or abrasive without notice, much like Betty's temperament. Both were incorrigible and seemed to have been similarly bred. I met Bill my first day I started working at St. Grace. He was a type of character not easily missed. He was very short and had a quirky personality. His dark hair was forever neatly trimmed crew cut style with just enough length to part and comb. He ran his mouth non-stop. I learned a lot about him within the first few minutes of our first encounter, like about his kidney problems, but he was sketchy on details. You see, he was mentally challenged, acted infantile all the time, and very snobbish like an ill-mannered brat. But mention food and Bill would be a very different man—articulate and demanding. Unfortunately, he was also a very picky eater, though living in an institution minimized his options. He ate what was on the menu. He never ceased to complain, but it always fell on deaf ears.

As I walked into Bill's room, I couldn't help, but think of how withdrawn, stubborn, and resentful of the burden of dialysis he had become. He no longer looked forward to going for his three weekly treatments. He didn't like being hooked-up on a machine, the chilliness of the room where the procedure took place, and chilling reaction of other patients at the treatment center. I hated going there too. He had once jokingly vowed to stop his treatment altogether. I knew he was not kidding. He saw no joy in a life lived in pain, assisted occasionally by a machine, and living in an institution.

That morning, Bill had one of his tri-weekly treatments. When I walked into his room, Bill was still in bed, which was unusual. His room smelled as fresh as always, scented with Airwick Lavender. He seemed to be in high spirits. His face beamed in smile and that cheered me up, making me forget the gloom of the morning.

"Good morning Bill," I said to him.

"Good morning Mary," he said with a smile.

"My! Oh, my," I said. "Someone is in a good mood this morning?"

"I am always good," he said jokingly. "You of all people should know I am always in a good mood."

"I am glad to know that," I said, moving away from his bed towards the window. I reached out for the blinds and pulled them open. "We have a long day today," I added, stealing a glance at him.

"I thought there are only twenty-hours in a day," he said with a smirk on his face. "Did you add more hours to elongate the day?"

"No . . . But am sure you know what I mean."

"No, I don't," he said. His mood was now changed from playful to serious.

"You know I have to take you for . . ."

"I am not going to that place again," he said affirmatively before I could complete my thought.

"You have to," I said calmly. "You know your life depends on it."

"You can't make me go if I don't want to . . . What happened to *freedom of choice?*" he said defiantly.

"You need the treatment for your own good," I said ignoring the part about freedom of choice. I understood all mortals' right and ability to choose, think, and act in a manner they deemed suitable to further their needs and for their own betterment. They deluded themselves of having the ability to control their destiny. Bill was no different. He deluded himself, too, believing he could control his destiny. Unfortunately, his situation was complicated. There were many others who held his destiny in the palm of their hands.

"I don't care what you say! I am not going . . . And that is that!" he said affirmatively.

"Can I at least get you ready?"

"No! You can't make me," his tone was icy. "It's not like I am asking for Jack Kevorkian to end my life."

"So long for a good morning!" I said exasperated.

I hurriedly walked out of Bill's room to find Joyce. I was certain, if anyone could talk some sense into him, it had to be her. Although he was of age and, under normal circumstances, he might have had the ability to make decisions that affected his life and well-being, his mental handicap impeded him. Unfortunately, I couldn't stop him from exercising his God given *right*, to choose what he deemed *right*. The outcome of his refusal to go for dialysis meant his death, a truth that didn't efface Bill. He saw nothing wrong with it, for he had come to terms with it a long time ago. Moreover, he had told me a couple weeks ago that he found no joy in living if his body couldn't function on its own, not assisted by the power of a machine. As I raced to the office, I knew Bill had a *right* to refuse his treatment, a *right* all mortals have, but his family had the final say.

At that time, my mind took flight to Papa, whom only weeks ago had been full of life . . . an alive and breathing organism. Now he was one with his ancestors, stone cold, and six feet under. I was still struggling to understand his demise only to be confronted by an enigma of a man determined to throw his life away much like Papa had done. And if you ask me, the whole thing sucked.

Annoyed, I wondered why, of all mornings, of all shifts, and of all days, Bill had chosen my morning, my shift, to stage his crazy protest. When I got to the office, I told Joyce about it. She was livid, of course and as I expected. It was as though I was behind Bill's refusal. She was wrong. She left right away to talk to Bill.

Unfortunately, nobody could change his mind, not even Joyce. He obstinately refused to go for dialysis. For he firmly believed it was the quality of life that mattered, not its prolongation. His life was not worthy of the machine upon which he was routinely hooked. "We all have to go sometime!" he said. "If I am okay with it. You, too, should be!"

How eventful the day turned out to be. All things considered, I completed my duties in stride—helping my clients with their basic needs: woke them up, cleaned them, aided those who needed help brushing teeth, bathed those who needed the assistance, changed linen on beds, and walked some to the dining room for breakfast. At lunch time, I fixed their meals. That was routine. I ran their afternoon errands. That, too, was routine. Before my shift came to an end, I logged my clients' daily activities in the logbook, which, too, was routine!

Joyce, Bill's doctor, the nurse, and his family couldn't change his mind . . . that was *freedom* of choice for you. Bill passed away shortly thereafter . . . not that same day, of course, but several months later!

17

When my shift ended, I walked out of St. Grace to my car as fast as light hoping to shake off the stress of the day. Outside, the air was cool and soothing. I closed my eyes and inhaled this freshness for a while. When I reopened them, the sky was a clear blue. What a beautiful spring evening. To the far west, the sun, a giant red globe, cast its golden glow upon earth. Its rays melted to the line where heaven touched earth. 'What a perfect evening,' I thought.

While I was still dazed, a red sedan Nissan driven by a middle-aged African woman approached the parking lot in full speed. She nearly struck me, but being light on my feet, I swiftly jumped out of her way. She turned off the engine of her car and hurriedly opened the door. She was such a petite woman. Before she stepped out of her car, I noticed that her feet dangled above ground. She was wearing white flat shoes, well suited for those who spent hours on their feet, and dressed in light blue scrubs. She didn't apologize to me for nearly knocking me over. I watched her as she quickened her pace to St. Grace. The doors flew open and closed behind her as she vanished behind them. I imagined what her evening would be like, but glad I wasn't her.

I made my way to my white Civic, my diamond, with ease. No sooner had I set foot inside than I started the engine and revved it. Surprisingly, Diamond didn't sound choked; instead, she purred softly. I locked my door, shifted her into gear, and let her slide off with ease from the parking lot.

I arrived home momentarily. I parked her in my usual spot, but I wasn't in a hurry to go inside as threats of my impending eviction returned. Before I stepped out of the car, I scanned the entire area to see if I could spot Sam Snackwell. A multitude of people were sitting outside on their porches. Some were drinking alcohol. I spotted a couple fiddling with their charcoal grill. The thought of grilled meat made my mouth water. Sam was nowhere in the vicinity. It was only then that I stepped out of Diamond and walked up the creaking stairs to my apartment. I quickly unlocked my door, swung it opened, and hurriedly walked inside. I bolted it immediately. Then I tossed my keys onto my kitchen counter and I headed straight for my couch where I collapsed. I didn't bother to turn on my lights or television. I sat there, in the dimness of light for hours, my mind consumed by Bill's apparent suicidal threat and Papa's suicide.

My mind also floundered to the role family must play in one's life, my life . . . and to Father and Mama Joy back home. They had been my strong supporters, my rock, unwavering in their dedication to me. I also thought of the role family played in my clients' lives. Hadn't some of them been abandoned at St. Grace? How different my world had been from the lives of Bill, Betty, and Cherry. They lived lonely lives even though they were surrounded by people. Mine wasn't any different from theirs . . . Maybe even worse, for I lived alone, away from my mother and father, and isolated from people. I couldn't help, but think of my clients' disconnection from *real* life experiences . . . little automatons lost at sea with limited to no control over their destinies—limited freedom of mobility and choice. I lived no better than them. I, too, was a lost soul and as lonely as they were, but with one difference: My alien status to American lifestyle made my plight more dismal.

As I thought about these things, I wondered what Mama Joy would have done had Bill been close of kin. Would she have taken him in her close enclaves or let him flounder in an institution? She, the fiery furnace of charity, a Mother Teresa of Kerongo. Certainly, she would have taken him in without doubt, following her conscience like she had done many times . . . No, many years with Grandma Tufroza.

I closed my eyes, again as my mind took flight away from Bill, away from Cherry, away from Betty, away from my neighbor Charlie, and away from Sam Snackwell. I shut them tightly and tightly, as I tumbled down and down, into the depth of my memory, to the sunny baked landscape of my homeland, through the desolate immensity of earth, sky, and water, to my village of Kerongo, where the land glistened and dripped with steam. I wanted to rest my tired body under the shade of the gum tree, just like I used to in my formative years. I wanted to guzzle-up a calabash full of cold water from *Ivugaywa* Spring . . . taste its freshness, not my chlorine tainted tap waters. I wanted to smell the spring freshness of home. Breathe in and out fresh air fragrant with sweet scents of flowers: bougainvillea. Jasmine. Daisies. Orchids. I wanted to run up-and-down the jagged Hills picking berries. Listen to the sounds of the wood-pecker pecking wood. Listen to crickets chirping in the middle of the night. Watch fireflies flapping their wings and flickering their lights on and off, on and off putting a glow to an already darkened sky. I wanted to sleep under the nightly dome, face-up. I wanted to search for the big dipper. I wanted to count the uncountable stars in the sky until I was exhausted with sleep. I wanted to wake up to a sunny baked rim of dawn on the eastern horizon dripping with light. I wanted to see the sun's orange rays spread across the skyline like a painting by an amateur artist. I tumbled farther and farther into reels of my past. A cool wind steered me farther into my bygone days as an image of my father emerged. He was a much older man now, much older than my own mother by two years, a woman whom he had married when he was twenty-three and she twenty-one.

My father, now seventy-two, was sitting under *my* shade on a clear blue day. He wasn't alone . . . I was with him. It was the way Mama Joy and I used to do. He was aloof. Ever present, but absent in my life. That was the Logooli way. Fathers lived under the shadowy present of their wives and children, while mothers shouldered the burden of rearing the children. They were as elusive as a ghost in a haunted house. Visible, but unseen, only making occasional appearance to halt children's boorishness or tomfoolery. Or decide their daughters' bride price. Other than that, a father, my father, to be precise, was a figurehead whom I dared not cross, but revered like a God. So, there he was with me . . . under the tree shade, sipping a freshly brewed cup of tea with his head tilted to the left. He, like Grandma Tufroza, was aged; his forehead was furrowed with countless folds of skin. I could tell because I was watching him from the corner of my eye. His head was bald save for the areas around his ears, reminding me that the old man once had hair. The thin line of hairs left on it had grayed. As he sipped his tea, beads of sweat began to glisten on his forehead. In his silence, I wondered what he was thinking. I couldn't ask him . . . it wasn't prudent for a child to intrude on a grown man's thoughts with foolish questions. I let him be . . .

As I watched him, thoughts of Mama Joy unfolded. I wondered if she ever fell in love with this old man. Really! The way a young girl falls in love with a boy, her heart pounding rapidly at seeing him. I wondered if she ever had sleepless nights thinking of him holding her hand. I wondered if she ever had thoughts of sneaking out of her grandmother's hut in the middle of the night just to see him. Or if he ever came to her window and tapped at it ever so gently seeking to gain entrance into her grandmother's hut to hold her abreast. I wondered if he was ever in love with her. For I never heard, for as long as I can remember, him tell her, 'I love you sweetheart!' or her return his sentiment, 'I love you too dear!' I dared not ask her or him; it was taboo. These words were absent in their lexicon. For love, the western style, didn't play a role in a Logooli woman's marriage. It was shown through deeds. I wondered how he proposed to her. No. He didn't. From the grapevine stories, my paternal grandpa went to my mother's home and made the proposal to her father. "I want your daughter for my son's wife." He must have added, "How many cows do you want in her exchange?" It must have been that simple. Mama Joy couldn't have accepted the proposal for marriage on her own. She was young . . . She didn't have a choice in the matter. Her father must have barked his order, "I have found a husband for you!" She complied like all dutiful girls. "He will make a good father for your children and your provider . . ."

My past, once more, intruded on my present to an incident that happened many years ago. It was after I had completed my form six exams in 1981. It was a warm sunny December mid-morning when we had very unusual visitors to our home. Mama and I were sitting under the canopy of the gum tree enjoying the day. Our free range chickens roamed about. Clucking hens hummed our joy scratching for bits of gravel in the grass. Our rooster joined in the humming with his crowing. Mother tasked me to chase away the neighbors' hens from feasting on our maize because we didn't have much going on that day. The harvest season was over and Mama Joy, our farm-hand boy, and I had just finished hauling loads of maize, spreading it out in the open to dry. Our compound was white as though covered in snow. This was an arduous back-breaking chore that lasted a couple of weeks following its shucking. It was then when we saw three women approach our compound.

Naturally, after we had exchanged formal greetings with our guests, Mama Joy sent me to the kitchen to start a fire to make them tea. She was very hospitable. Being tired, I went begrudgingly. Not because I didn't want to make the tea for our visitors, but I hated the process of doing it. It was painstaking. Looking for dry firewood to start the fire was a painful chore. Out of respect, I dared not question Mama; it was my responsibility. Mama walked our visitors into the main house, while I went reluctantly into the kitchen. No sooner had I gotten there than I made for the stove. With a piece of wood, I poked into the stove. Hot embers of the morning fire still sizzled. I broke pieces of wood, laid it above red hot embers and started fanning the fire with a plate; swirling ash particles spiraled up into open space. Thick dark smoke spiraled upwards filling the room. Choked with smoke, I sneezed. My eyes began to itch and my nose was transformed into a stream. I wiped my nose dry with the sleeve of my blouse. I fanned and fanned the fire for a minute before it burst into flames. I moved away from the stove, getting ready to fetch water for the tea. Suddenly, I heard a ruckus from the main house. I abandoned my mission and ran outside to see what was going on . . .

What I saw bemused me. The women, with whom Mama had moments before walked into the main house, were running out in screams. Mama, running after them with a broom in hand, was yelling, "Leave my home this very minute and don't you ever come back here again with your foolishness!" she said, waggling the broom threateningly at them . . . That was the only time, to my recollection, Mama Joy was uncivil to another human being. Whatever they had said to her must have irked her very much.

"Mama Joy we were simply sent to you!" one of the women, Phanice, protested as she walked swiftly away from Mama to avoid being flogged. "You shouldn't be cross with the messenger," she said. The woman's words simply fell on Mama's deaf ears.

"I don't care who sent you here, don't you dare come back again! You hear me?" The women were too frightened to offer a response. "Who told you my daughter wants to get married?" she raved.

What a thrilling spectacle! I was glad the women left before I had time to make them tea . . . It saved me the hassle of preparing it and cleaning afterwards.

When the women were long gone, Mama walked back to the tree shade where she sat in silence for a very long time. I joined her there and sat by her side. I hoped she would tell me which of my sisters was the one for whom the unusual proposal had been made. She never did and I didn't press her for details. I knew, with time, she would tell me. Several days later, she spoke to my sister in-law who wrote to her sister in the USA who then sent me application forms for admission from a couple of universities. I applied to both and received admission from both. So here I am . . .

Months later, when I was getting ready for my travel to America, she reminded me of the incident.

"Do you remember the three women who came here not long ago?"

I wasn't thinking about the incident. I had long forgotten it. "Which women?" I said.

"Those I chased away from here!"

"Oh, yes! . . . Those ones," I said, my mind taking flight to Mama running after the women with a broom in her hand. She was such a frightful sight.

"Do you know why I chased them?"

"No!" I said. "You never told me."

"They had come to ask for your hand in marriage."

"Oh!" I gasped.

"Do you know why I kicked them out of my house?"

"No!"

"To give you a *chance* in life . . . A chance I never had!"

"Oh!" I said.

"I had no dreams of my own those days," she said. "My life's path had been predestined from birth—to be a wife and mother."

I was flabbergasted to say the least. I didn't know how to respond to Mama's revelation.

"Yes! You have an opportunity to make a difference in your life. I wished I had the same."

There was a sparkle in her eyes. Mama's truth warmed my spirits. I saw the same twinkle I saw in her eyes the day I received my admission letters to college. Only that time, the sparkle was magnified tenfold. It penetrated into the depth of my heart and warmed my spirit. No embrace was necessary. Only a meaningful silence followed and remained. She didn't ask me if I wanted to get married or go to school. It wasn't my decision to make, but I was glad she did what she did. Mama had her best interests of me at heart. I knew Mama's dream of education was fulfilled in me. And for that I am forever indebted to her ...

As I sat, still curled-up on my couch, my mind catapulted around the globe, soaring in a big two-winged bird that glides the cloudy skies, and boomeranged me back to a rapt and hearty laughter of female voices. The women were heading towards Charlie's apartment. Right away, I knew who they were. Their shrill-giggly voices were very distinct. I wondered if they had snuffed something. To drown their voices, I flipped on my television.

The girls had become Charlie's regular visitors. The more they came to see him, the less frequent his visits to my home become. The 'old' Charlie never failed to come into my apartment to say a simple 'hello.' Not anymore. If he dared to show-up, he simply peeked into my door claiming, "Mary, I am going out with the girls tonight!" And with the tip of his hat, he would vanish as quickly as he appeared. I wondered if I should be worried about him, but I had no just cause. He had simply taken the girls into his bosom as though they were his longtime friends. Unbeknownst to them, as he had made known to me, Charlie had one mission for them: to convert the girls into viable heterosexuals.

Unfortunately, the girls were too loud that I continued to still hear their laughter above the deafening sound of my television. I tried time and again to block their voices out of mind, but I couldn't. Perhaps, it wasn't because they were loud, but my envy of their carefree lifestyle. They were not alone. Though, maybe there was a logical reason for envying them. Maybe they were not burdened by any financial constraints like me. As new Somali immigrants to the US, they relied on subsidies from Uncle Sam: Free housing, food stamps, and health benefits. Unlike them, I had a host of problems: my eminent eviction, lack of food, and being flat broke all the time. These factors magnified my isolation. I never used to be like that . . . I used to find joy in the company of other people. Socializing was the madness with which I sought anchorage in my life and occasionally sipping a glass of long island ice tea.

Several hours later, when my stomach suddenly began to churn for food, I walked to my refrigerator, pulled out my leftovers from two days ago, nuked them in my microwave, and returned onto my couch to eat while I watched Jeopardy followed by Wheel of Fortune. As I nibbled on my food, I could still hear the hearty laughter from Charlie's apartment. The laughter rose and fell to Alex Trebek reading a question from the "Anti" Category: "A let down or disappointing conclusion." One of the contestants' buzzed in, saying, "Anti-climax!" He was right.

I was suddenly startled from the show by sounds of light-lady-like footsteps of a person ascending the stairs. I knew the footsteps couldn't have been Sam's because his were heavy with bravado like swagger of a man seeking recognition. I knew they weren't the girls because they were already in Charlie's apartment, drinking beer and smoking cigarettes. The footsteps were girlish, soft and delicate, as though she was afraid of breaking the heels of her shoes. Even our creakily stairs made soft low-keyed squeaking sounds. I stopped eating and peered through the window to see who it was. Because my lights were off, I watched her unabashed.

On closer examination, I realized it wasn't a lady walking up the stairs, but a young man deftly dressed in brown corduroy jeans with a cream-colored shirt tailored to fit. He was dressed to kill. He reminded me of a beautiful woman I had seen in a club one summer in Cincinnati. The moment my eyes caught a glimpse of him, my heart skipped a beat, for I had never seen such a fine womanish man. From where I was, I could only see his back. His curly hair was trimmed short.

When he got to Charlie's apartment, he gently tapped on his door. Then, he stood in wait for admittance. There was no answer. He knocked again. Still there was no answer. He turned his head and looked in my direction. That was when I saw his face. He was the most beautiful man I had ever seen. He was fair skinned with baby-like facial features. His hair was brushed to the back exposing his bushy eyebrows. Suddenly, I felt uneasy about watching him, wondering if he had spotted me. It was hard to tell. He turned again and faced Charlie's door. He knocked a third and fourth time before the door flew open. Charlie was all smiles to see him. The man walked in and Charlie pulled the door shut behind him. Immediately, I lost my appetite for food, developing a desire for something more elusive and much greater than food. Like a person possessed, I wanted to meet that chap. Without thinking, the word "Damn" softly slipped off my lips. "How could God waste such beauty on a man? He should have been a woman!"

Determined to meet this fellow, I jumped off my couch, and headed straight for the door, only to stop midway. I couldn't let him see me the way I looked. I was still lousily dressed in my work clothes and looked haggard. The man was dressed in style and I knew he couldn't give a ramshackle girl like me a moment of his time. Without thinking, as though I had lost my rational faculties, I abandoned my dinner altogether, and ran for the shower, convinced a quick rinse would cure my quirkiness.

I was out of my clothes in pronto. Within no time, I was standing under the soothing gushy waters of my shower, cleansing my body, from head to toe, of the nauseating smells of St. Grace. I closed my eyes soothed by the needle-poking spray of my shower for a very long time. Turning off the shower, I quickly dried my body, put on my borrowed face, masked under my Fashion Fair soufflé make-up, delicately arched my eye-brows with a charcoal eye-liner, and with my brown lip-liner, I drew a thin arched line on my soft curved lips. Right above the line, I added a thin layer of a purple lipstick to highlight my lips. Within an interval of three minutes, I was now looking at an image of a transformed young beautiful Kenyan woman. She was staring back at me, smiling admiringly at herself and throwing me a long drawn-out French kiss.

I walked out of the bathroom to my bedroom looking for an outfit that would accentuate my looks. As Mama Joy always said, "Young lady . . . kid not yourself, you are what you wear!" Dark clothing was out of the question. I wasn't in mourning. I wanted a bright dazzling attire that would make my face glow. Nonetheless, I didn't have a variety of clothes in my wardrobe, but that was okay.

"Jeans. Yes. Jeans. That is it," I said with a hidden delight. I could wear my hip-huggers, flared-low-cut corduroy jeans, the only brand-name jeans in my possession: Tommy Hilfiger and curved around my body perfectly. Without wasting time, I reached into my closet, pulled out my pair. Sitting at the edge of my bed, I thrust my feet in, pulling them all the way to my waistline. They stopped just slightly below my navel. My bare navel made me wish I had pierced it. I bet it would have been dazzling to dangle a long gold ring in it. I walked back to my closet, took out my sexy-low-cut red blouse, and draped it around my upper body; it fit perfectly like a glove. I walked back into the bathroom, to steal a second look at my amiable self. I smiled at the stunning image of a girl gazing back into my eyes. As I was about to walk out of the bedroom, I realized I hadn't put on any jewelry. Again, I walked back into the room, drew open my drawer, pulled out a red matching set of my Masai beaded earrings and necklace to complement my outfit. I emerged out of my bedroom as Alex Trebek was announcing the final category: Business. I paused to listen to the final jeopardy question. "This company founded in 1945 offers a special deal on the last day of January, March, May, July, August, October, and December," he said. I stood in wait for the thirty seconds contestants are expected to write their answer. The first contestant missed. Not the second. He wrote down the correct answer, "What is Baskin Robbins?" I turned off my T.V.

As I was just about to head for Charlie's apartment, I noticed all his lights were out and it was as dark as the charcoal etched sky over our building. I froze in my tracks as the blustery sounds of my neighbors' televisions rent the air. Younger folks blasted their stereos with music so loud they deserved to be cited for disturbing the peace. In my naiveté and eagerness, of craving the impossibility, I forgot one thing—to check in with Charlie. Thus, the very excitement that had sent me racing into the shower, was gone in a rupture of a second. In its place, a searing hollowness settled in my heart and remained. Charlie and his companions must have gone out for the night. Feelings of disappointment came over me like an avalanche. I walked back to my couch where I sat feeling my brokenness as life's sorrows cradled my soul. I had no presence of mind to take off my shoes or change into my pajamas. I sat there . . . on my couch . . . I turned on the T.V. as I withdrew into the depth of my past. I didn't bother to turn on my lights or draw my blinds.

Moments later, I curled my body on my couch, buried my head in its corner and wrapped my body in my heavy fluffy comforter. I shut my eyes tightly, leaving my ears attuned to the booming sound of Pat Sajak's voice as he announced his show's theme. "It is ultimate adventure week on Wheel of Fortune. Location—Hawaii Island!" Unfortunately, I could barely erase the events of the day off my mind . . . Bill and his suicide threat to the image of the young man who had awakened in me impulses of a yearning desire for human companionship. It was natural . . . innately human. In my aloneness and loneliness, I craved the warmth of human touch . . . maybe a kiss.

Only then did I begin to think of what I would have said to him had we met. *Perhaps, I would have been the first to approach him? Maybe say to him, "Good afternoon sir!" Maybe I would wait for him to answer. Maybe have him greet me first.*

'My name is Mary Upanga.' No. I would have said, 'Pardon me Sir! You look very familiar. Have we met before?' a mischievous smile hanging loosely on my face.

'No! You must be mistaking me for someone else. I just arrived from Aruba a few weeks ago.' Or he would have said, 'Oh yes! I remember you,' a half-baked smile appearing on his face. 'I met you three weeks ago at Mr. X's graduation party. My name is Jay.'

Elated, I move my hand to shake his, 'My name is Mary. Mary Upanga.' I feel the warmth of his hand between mine after making our first human contact.

No. What if Charlie introduced us? That would be the most natural way.

"My friend Mr. X!" Charlie says, "This is my Mary . . . Mary Upanga!"

I pushed these thoughts off my mind, above the loud turning wheel of the game show, remembering I was "dressed for a night out," but I had nowhere to go. Soon sadness again came crushing upon me, erasing every other emotion of my being. There was no love, joy, or laughter; instead, an aching hollowness found its permanence in my heart and remained.

I thought of going to Club Zanzibar, where Charlie and his friends might have gone, but I changed my mind. I had no money to pay the entrance charge. I couldn't afford to buy a drink either. The truth of my being broke was as depressing as the hollowness of my heart. There wasn't much I could do to change that truth save from working hard. If ever there was something I could change, it was my gambling. It was a self-destructive behavior. Only a few people were lucky enough to strike it rich. I wasn't one of those people. I heard a story of Ugandan man who won five millions, but squandered most of it on frivolous things—cars. A large mansion. Women. Who could forget women? They, perceived as cause of man's fall. Having been dealt a wicked hand, I knew the lottery wasn't for me. I pushed these thoughts off my mind once more, awakened to my pulsing present by the wide turning Wheel of Fortune the show. "Three hundred dollars," Sajak said.

"Is there a T," a contestant said.

"There are two Ts," Sajak said.

I opened my eyes only to see a radiant Vanna White, immaculately dressed in a full length sleeveless black gown that sparkled under the television light. What a striking contrast to my corduroy jeans and red shirt. She walked gracefully onto the board to reveal the letters.

The wheel spun to a contestant's push . . . "Big money! Big money!"

"Nine hundred dollars," Sajak said.

"Is there a W?"

"Yes, there is one W!" Vanna walked to the board, revealed the W, as the contestants once more said, "I would like to buy a vowel please . . . an A." A buzzer went off. Sajak spun the wheel for the last time.

I closed my eyes just as Vanna was revealing another letter, cutting my link from the world of television . . .

When I woke up hours later, the night was half-spent. My T.V was still on, but I couldn't tell the time. I squinted my eyes adjusting them to the dullness of light in my room. Then, I shifted my gaze from the television to my wide-open living room window. Outside, the night's blanket of darkness wrapped the earth in its tender embrace concealing the moon's glory from view. Every so often, the moon fought hard against this blackness, a blackness which was broken by the hazy security light at the corner of Charlie's apartment. Through this hazy glow, the imposing darkness in Charlie's apartment remained. I crawled out of my couch, one foot at a time, and walked towards the window to draw my blinds determined to cut my connection to the world.

I reached out for the wand to close my blinds, but I was distracted by something greater than life. Way up in the night sky, the moon slowly glided behind the clouds above the sleeping immensity of earth. Inside was an image of a human form. It was neither male nor female. Mesmerized, my mind moved in many directions. I tried to understand its characteristics . . . How the moon glides so swiftly above the starry sky. Or does it? Was it the moon which rotated around the earth or the other way around? I remembered what my science teacher once told us in class . . . That the moon appeared to rotate the earth each day, but it was the earth's rotation, which gave that appearance. If the moon didn't rotate, it must be in the same position.

Filled with awe and wonder, I pinned my face onto the window's cold glassy surface and watched the moon until it completely vanished behind the clouds and darkness fell upon earth once more. I drew my blinds and slowly walked to my bedroom. I disrobed and put on my pajamas. I walked back into my living room and, once again, I wrapped my body under the comforter as though I never left its comfort.

With a remote in hand, I flipped channel after channel looking for a good show or movie to tame my interest, but there was hardly anything interesting. Disappointed, I closed my eyes as past intruded my present . . .

My mind and soul were transposed to a faraway world . . . my sunny baked landscape of Kerongo with the sun at its zenith. I was sitting under the canopy of the gum tree again dreaming about being by the lake shore side. There the blue sky and its giant ball of fire glided above me with ease, reflected in a mirror-like-stillness of

Lake Victoria. I was alone surrounded with an overwhelming sense of peacefulness. I could hear the whistling wind sway tree leaves above me. Chirping birds, hidden from my view, sang melodious tunes of hope.

Mama Joy appeared before me. She was so real. I could almost touch her. We were both sitting at our special place . . . The Gum Tree. She was looking at me as though she was seeing me for the first time. Her eyes were staring at me stonily . . . No, they gazed stonily past me and uphill towards Maragoli hills, all the way to *Engonono,* a magical rock curved like bow, at the zenith of the hills. A place where people went to offer sacrifices to the gods. I, too, followed her eyes with my own. She was as happy as she could be. Soon, I was distracted by something. No. It is someone. I could see Grandma Tufroza making another visit to our home and I knew what that visit meant. She wasn't alone. I saw another person with her. No. Two people. They were not strangers, but invaders to our space, *my* space with Mama Joy. They were sipping hot tea under the tree shade while the heat of the hot December month sizzled. They had important matters to discuss . . . Otherwise, why would two men be sitting under the tree shade in the middle of the day. Okay. It was my Uncle Keya, my father's older brother, and he had come to talk to him about my impending journey to America. Mama Joy and I were with them, but we were merely spectators . . . Women weren't allowed a voice in such matters. I was no woman. Just a girl unsure of life.

My Uncle Keya believed it pointless to educate girls. It was even more pointless if the journey for my education involved leaving home to some unknown world.

"It is double tragedy if you ask me!" he tells Father. I remembered his voice vividly. His sadistic voice importuned my father not to even consider my education.

"My brother . . . I tell you," Keya said, moving his hand to his chin as though he were deeply in thought. "You shouldn't let Upanga go to America. That land is unknown to us, to our ancestors. You shouldn't let your daughter go, *our* daughter! What good will education do her?"

My father didn't say a word. He just sat there letting his brother echo sentiments already expressed by most of my relatives, male and female alike. These relatives lacked gumption to express their views to Father face-to-face. Instead, they whispered privately, but my father got wind of it nonetheless. I was certain my Father would fold under their belligerence.

"If you let her go, you might as well as count her dead!" Keya added.

That was harsh. Real harsh, I remember thinking then. The finality implied in the word *dead* wasn't something I had considered. Education was supposed to be good. I turned to my mother, but she, like my father, was soundless. I wondered what was going through her mind. I dared not ask her about it. It was impolite. Puppy eyed, I turned to my uncle, begging him not to interfere in my life. I begged him with my eyes, hoping to halt his tirade about the perils of education, or his desire to change my father's mind . . . Or going against the whispery voices of my relatives' displeasure with my academic pursuit. He didn't. Instead he ignored me.

"Your daughter . . . *Our* daughter will return to us spoiled . . . Her innocence ravaged by unknown men. My brother, do not let *our* daughter go away." Father listened with curious intensity, but remained soundless.

"Let her attend Nairobi University or Kenyatta University. There is nothing wrong with these institutions." Again, Father was soundless.

"She will return to us as *kidwaadi,* her womb flushed off unwanted life," Keya argued. My father didn't seem to be hearing him or if he did, he didn't give himself away.

When he had said his peace, my uncle left. As for my father, he had already decided to let me go. Going against his brother's wishes, going against all my relatives, he cut me loose, hopeful in my future success. He gave me a chance many girls in the village lacked . . . freedom to experience life. Be myself. Make my own mistakes. Fall and rise with every error I make. And, I must confess, I have made plenty of errors . . .

I was reeled back to my pulsing present with loud thumping footsteps of people ascending our creaky stairs. Charlie and his friends must have been coming home. I recognized him by the sound of his voice. I recognized his heavy footsteps crushing hard against the squeaky stairs. I recognized the familiar voices of his companions. Within no time, I heard the jiggling of Charlie's keys as he pushed it into the door. He must have turned the key to the right. I heard the familiar screeching sound as his door flew open and fell back behind them. That was the last thing I heard before I went to bed.

As I pulled my covers above my head that night, I fell asleep to Mama Joy's parting words, "My daughter go to America and be our eyes and ears." I remembered the warmth of her breath around my nape as she tightly hugged and bid me goodbye at the airport. I collapsed in her bosom as I struggled to hold back tears. As I walked away from her, there was a giant choking lump in my throat. I moved my right hand to feel my neck as though Mama's warmth was frozen there in a time capsule . . .

18

The next morning I woke up at the twilight of dawn. I didn't rush out of bed. I laid there until the sunlight dazzled the eastern hemisphere. It was Friday and pay day. I knew I would have Sam Snackwell's rent and glad he didn't show at my doorstep as he had threatened, *"I will be back tomorrow and you better have my rent. . . . Or else!"* As I laid there, I could hear his menacing voice in my mind's eye, a crispy clear voice. I saw him coming after me through the mist of my tranquil morning, only to disrupt it as he pinched my shoulder until giant marks of his nails were engraved in my flesh. Then, he vanished as the sun's golden glow shone brilliantly into my room through the cracks in my drapes. I got out of bed, dropped on my knees, and prayed for strength and courage. I also prayed for Divine intervention even though I knew prayers alone, without action, weren't sufficient. Still, I put my fate in His hands and hoped to keep a positive mind the entire day.

I got out of bed after a while and took time with my morning rituals: I showered, got dressed, and put on make-up. I enjoyed a nice cup of my hot morning coffee. It was my favorite sweet aromatic creamy hazelnut latte. Within no time, I was off to the car. As I headed for work, I dreaded what awaited me, but the sun's brilliant glow, though blinding, made everything seem alright. Its rays above a cloudless sky had the appearance of a flower whose petals illuminated earth with its glow. 'What a beautiful morning,' I thought. Unfortunately, the thought of awaiting monotony of my daily grind clamped my joy. It wasn't so much the physical challenge of the job, but the emotional test to survive another day was what made it daunting and deserved courage. If a client refused to comply with the norm, like Bill had previously, everything snowballed into a series of many unexpected events. This reality filled me with trepidation.

I arrived at work on time. As always, the stale hospital-like smell of St. Grace ambushed me. This smell no longer bothered me, for it had become norm. I kept my chin-up while at work aware there was no dawn that didn't end at dusk, and no hurdle so high I couldn't overcome! You might say, I was like that *The Little Engine That Could!* I was certain I was destined to survive another day. As fate would have it, my morning was incident free, with a few minor hiccups here and there, but not too much to dampen my spirits. Bill was still grouchy and adamantly refused to go for treatment. Betty seemed to be perky and Cherry was cheery as usual.

When my shift ended, I returned home at dusk to a chilly apartment, but I couldn't lose sight of my earlier resolve to be positive. Naturally, sulking was out of the question for the evening. I had some cash in my pocket. I was going to buy food . . . real food from Kroger before the day's end. I wanted to buy chicken drumsticks, collard greens (with bouillon cubes for seasoning), and a five pound bag of white corn flour for *ugali*—corn meal. My mouth watered just thinking about it. I had not eaten *ugali* in a very long time. Pacifying my hunger on it would be splendid, but I had no urgency to go to Kroger. Instead, I changed out of my work clothes and sat down to watch one or two late afternoon shows. I hadn't done that kind of thing in a very long time. I had only two options in mind: Ellen or the Oprah Winfrey's show. I opted for the Oprah Show. I didn't know what she had on that afternoon, but I wished it was something uplifting. I flipped my T.V. on and switched the channel from NBC to CBS. A Palmolive dish washing soap commercial came on. 'Aah! Just what I need!" I said. I sat down and waited for the program to begin.

Meanwhile, a strange idea crept onto my mind. What if I send Oprah a letter, or an e-mail soliciting her help? The idea hit me hard like a brick! Yes. That is it! What if I wrote her a letter? I could title it: Help a Kenyan Girl Realize Her Dream! That is it. What a catchy and interesting idea. It was precise and onto the point. For precision was key. That's it! I wanted to realize my Dreams. Hadn't she aided many singers find and sign contract deals with recording companies? Hadn't she helped a young girl recently find her dream as a cover girl model? Hadn't she provided many folks, through her *Oprah's Angel Network*, improved the lives of downtrodden souls of the world? Hadn't she provided a voice to many black women . . . Not just black women, but women in general? Women who saw no hope in life? What would hinder her from aiding me? I was in need! I needed school fees. I needed clothing. I needed food. I needed shelter! Those were *my real* needs! As these thoughts ran through my mind like the wind, a passage Father used to read to us in our younger years from the Holy Book flashed, "Ask and it will be given to you; seek and you will find; knock and the door will be opened to you. For everyone who asks receives; the one who seeks finds; and to the one who knocks, the door will be opened!" I couldn't recall from whence the passage came, but there it was! As clear as a bell. The embodiment of all my wants and desires. No. My thoughts.

Before I could act on my thoughts, I was distracted by the ringing sound of my telephone. I contemplated not answering it, but the ringing persisted: Briiingg! Briiingg! Briiingg! The telephone rang again. For a fraction of a second, my brain was frozen as though dipped in a bucket of ice. The sound stopped for a minute. I heaved a sigh of relief, but it was a short lived relief. Before I could dig deep for my lost thoughts, the phone rang again: Briiingg! Briiingg! Briiingg! The monstrosity nagged me to my wits end with its intrusiveness as it rang again for the third, fourth, and fifth time. Ultimately, I decided to answer it, hoping the caller would leave me once and for all. I didn't have a caller ID on my phone. I would have censored my calls. When I finally answered, it was Charlie! I wasn't surprised. I had suspected it would be him. That was why I was reluctant to reach for the receiver. Granted, I had not spoken to him for a very long time . . . At least, not the way we used to talk. He now had other interesting buddies than me and I had no time, for idle chitchat, since I had to work long hours to make ends meet.

"Hi Mary," came his voice from the other end of the line.

"Charlie, is that you?" I said. "What have you been up to lately?

"Not much," he said. His voice sounded raspy. I could sense some sadness in his tone.

"Is everything okay with you?"

"Well!" he paused for a second. "Are you busy right now?"

"Not really," I said, wondering why he wanted to know. I knew if Charlie came to see me, I would not be able to write my letter to

Oprah. He always had impressive tall tales to tell. There was no telling how long it would take him to complete narrating one. Or how much of my time he was going to take from my evening.

"Alright then!" he paused for a second. "May I come over and talk to you?" There was a sense of urgency in his tone.

Naturally, my mind began to race in different directions. I wondered if something bad had happened to Charlie. The last time he had insisted he wanted to talk to me was when Papa died . . . Maybe, he had finally decided to go back to school. It was the only thing he routinely spoke of. Or perhaps he had finally found love. It was not out of question. Hadn't he once told me he wanted to settle down, even if he had no girlfriend? If that were the case, then surely he was a lucky dog! Or could he have succeeded in converting his gay lady friends into a viable heterosexual? It had to be *it*. I couldn't think of anything else other than *it*.

"Sure Charlie," I said. "Come on over!" I replaced my receiver and waited.

Soon, I heard a soft tapping sound on my door. I rose from my couch, walked to the door and unlocked it. The door flew-open. Right before me, stood a much disheveled Charlie. His light blue shirt was creased and his hair looked unkempt as though it had made a do not comb pact with a hair brush. His eyes were red hot like cayenne pepper, a sign he may have not slept for days. It wasn't characteristic of Charlie to be disheveled. I wondered what had befallen him.

"Are you okay Charlie," I said, leading him into my living room.

"I guess I am okay," he said. I didn't believe him.

"May I make you some tea?" I said even though I knew Charlie didn't drink tea. His drink of choice was beer . . . any beer. Red Stripe. Old English. Colt 45. Guinness. You name it, he drank it indiscriminately. The only time I saw him with a hot beverage was long time ago. It was winter time and understandably so. He had been outside shoveling snow when the cold got to him. It was so cold his blood ran cold through his veins. His bones, too, were chilled. This was the kind of chillness Red Stripe couldn't cure. On that day, he drank a steaming cup of coffee to warm himself.

"I only have tea in this house to drink! No *pombe—beer*—my brother," I said. Charlie didn't answer.

"It is Kenyan tea—fresh from Kericho!" I said.

"Sure Mary! I will try your Kenyan tea," he said getting ready to sit down. As I walked to my kitchenette to make the tea, Charlie sat down looking glum. His personal affect spoke volumes. There he was, a man who seemed to be carrying the world's burdens on his shoulders.

"The remote is on the table," I said. "You can turn on the T.V. if you would like while I make us some tea."

"No. . . I don't feel like watching T.V.!"

It didn't take me long to make the tea . . . five minutes to be precise. I walked back to the living room, set the two mugs of steaming tea on my coffee table next to the T.V. guide, sat down facing Charlie and anxiously awaited his story. His head was downcast. He appeared so flustered I could barely guess what had happened to him. Not wanting to intrude on his private thoughts, I shifted my focus from Charlie to my window that faced his apartment. Slants of silver light streamed in through my wide open drapes. I moved my eyes away from the window to the table.

Cyclical shafts of steam spiraled from our tea cups. I watched the steam coil up until it vanished into open space. Charlie was still quiet. He was so quiet that it was discomforting.

Without thinking, I reached for my tea cup and began to slowly sip on it. It was sweet, warm, and comforting. Charlie watched me for a fraction of a second, and then, unexpectedly, he said, "My sister Mary!" he fell silent again and took a prolonged sigh.

"I lost my identity last night!"

"What do you mean?" I said.

"My sister! . . . I lost my identity last night!"

"By golly Charlie, what are you talking about?"

He fell quiet again! Everything became still. I, too, was still. As still as the air between us. Outside, the sun was now covered with massive clouds. I couldn't tell if it would rain.

"Yeah! My Sister . . . oo! I lost it all *my* sister. I lost it all last night!"

"Charlie, you are not making sense. Take a deep breath and then tell me what happened. All of it, from the beginning to finish," I said.

"I intend to," he said. He picked his teacup from the table and took a few sips in a slow and deliberate manner. "It all happened last night," he began, but paused abruptly. He took another sip of his tea before he continued.

"You know, I went out with my Somali friends last night. The two girls. The ones I told you about!"

"Yes," I said, remembering how sad I was I had not met the young man the previous night.

Another prolonged moment of silence lapsed. I picked my cup again and took two small sips. The tea was sweetly spiced with ginger and tea masala, but extremely hot so I went easy on it. I couldn't rush this kind of goodness. Charlie's cup was back on the table now. Steam from it spiraled upwards and vanished into thin air. I put my cup back onto the table just as Charlie broke into a rant:

"My Sister! Believe it or not," he said. "Yesterday, I kissed a boy. No. He was not a boy . . . I mean! I kissed a man!"

"What?"

"Oh! His musk scented body was very inviting. No. It was a cross between musk and cashmere mist."

As those words fell off Charlie's lips, my jaw fell open. Unexpectedly, I experienced a sharp pain crop around my temples. They throbbed as though they were being tightly wrung like a wet rug. I moved my hands to my temples and began to massage them in circular motion with my stiffened fingers. I said absolutely nothing, stupefied by a truth so insidious I was muted by it. This was a very uncharacteristic demeanor for me. Charlie understood my silence and watched me in silence. The expressions on my face must have spoken louder than any words I could have expressed. I don't know if it was a disapproving look.

"Really, I did! He was a beautiful handsome looking man. Tall, smooth-faced, fair-skinned, and had a dimple on his left cheek. His face glowed in my dimly lit lights. When he walked into my apartment last night, I thought, 'Gee-Wheeze! Holy-Mother of God!' What a beauty! Then it hit me . . . It had to . . . The unquenchable desire you know."

The man Charlie was describing was the very man I had seen last night ascending the stairs into his apartment. He was deftly dressed in his corduroy jeans. Only that I hadn't been close enough to observe intricate details of his physique like Charlie had. All I remember were the soft and stealth nature of his footsteps as he walked up the stairs. So faint were they that had he been a woman, she might have been afraid to break the heels of her *stiletto* shoes.

"His name is Aboud," Charlie said slowly, allowing this name to slip softly off his lips, dazed like a man infatuated by a girl he knows he cannot have. "His hair is curly and trimmed short and appeared golden brown under the dim lights of my apartment. He is from Somalia . . . A new immigrant of not long ago. You remember recently when the government relocated many folks from that region . . . Right Mary! He wasn't among the first wave of immigrants of 1996. He has been here for a couple of years." I nodded in agreement. "Yes, he just came here recently. I lost *it* . . . My sense of direction as I looked at him. Next thing I knew me, Sophie and her girlfriend Zainabu, Aboud and I were sitting in Club Zanzibar sipping on gin and tonic. I drank too much. I drank more than I ever do. I didn't know myself . . . I lost my identity," he fell silent again, enough to let me commit to memory what he had just told me. His head was tilted to the floor, as though he was afraid to look into my eyes lest I judge him for '*the* immoral' sin he had just committed.

Unbeknownst to Charlie, I couldn't judge him! How could I? I was no saint. I was just as sinful as any other person in this world. Right then and there, drip-by-drip, one of Father's stories from the Holy Book, once more, intruded on my present. It was a story of Mary Magdalene whom the Son of God had defended in his uttered famous statement, *Let he who is without sin cast the first stone*. I couldn't cast a stone at Charlie's impropriety.

"We must have been at Club Zanzibar for about two to three hours. When we returned home, the lights in your apartment were out. I had wanted to come in and see you, but I couldn't. I was buzzed . . . You know, with all the gin and tonic."

Charlie was quiet again. I was glad he didn't come to my house last night.

"Someone slipped me a *mickey*! That is it. Someone must have slipped me a *mickey*! How could I have lost my mind?" Charlie said remorsefully. I didn't say anything in response even if I knew Charlie was begging my encouragement.

Sweat began to form on Charlie's brow. "I mean really! Someone put something in my drink," he added trying effortlessly to convince me of a logical reason as to what might have happened . . . A mere physical attraction he may have felt for the man defied logic. Charlie's logic. My logic, but I couldn't tell him I agreed with his rationalization.

"When we came back to my apartment, I fixed more drinks . . . I don't even remember how many glasses we guzzled. Sophie and Zainabu were sitting on my love seat while Aboud and I took the couch. We were all drinking you know! Talking and laughing and making merry. You know the way I like to have a good time!"

I nodded my agreement.

"Aboud moved closer to me as though he was about to say something to me, but he didn't; instead, he held my hand, squeezed it a little, and I couldn't resist reciprocating his soft grasp. Then, everything about me began to twirl. The warm feeling inside of me. That warmth of being held you know."

"I like you!" he said.

"I like you too," I said, sounding rather juvenile in the manner with which our simple *innocent* words fell off our lips. He moved close to me; I moved close to him. In that moment, in my mind, I didn't see a man, but a beautiful woman with short trimmed hair. She held my hand and I held hers. My heart was pounding so hard against my rib-cage. I was certain she could hear its pounding. I was gone . . . Lost in the tenderness of that moment . . . Her soft warm hands. I was totally bushed. My head moved slowly towards her shoulder without any provocation. Resting it gently on her shoulder, I felt contented. She felt contented for she didn't protest at all. Neither did I. It was a simple human to human attraction. I closed my eyes allowing the self within to be carried away. She moved her lips towards mine. They locked. There was a ringing silence between us as though nothing else mattered in the world, in *our* world. She began to kiss me very passionately and I couldn't say a damn thing to stop her. How could I? I was complacent, enjoying as much as she was. Ultimate bliss. Feelings of mutuality. We were not alone. Sophie and Zainabu were in the same room with us. It didn't matter! She had transported me to a world I hadn't been in a very long time. We moved our escapade to my bedroom."

Charlie fell silent. It must have been the strange expression on my face that caused him to stop . . . One of utter disbelief and, perhaps, disgust, both intertwined.

What had happened to Charlie? Where was my brother, Charlie the womanizer? How did he expect me to accept such news? Good thing he hadn't sworn me into secrecy! I wouldn't have shared his story with you. I knew Charlie. He wasn't gay or bisexual, at least, so I thought. Now, I could no longer vouch for his being straight given he had yielded to sexual temptation. Or could it have been an act of the Down Low, of men whose public identification is straight, but who have discreet sex with other men outside of their primary relationship? I couldn't explain it. Even as I tell you now, I can't come to grips with that truth of Charlie, my brother and friend, kissing a man and hadn't known it was a man whom he had kissed. And had enjoyed every moment of it.

"We kissed some more," Charlie continued. I felt her hand slipping down towards my pants, and she was gently sliding my zipper off!" Charlie paused. "I drank too much. I lost myself! I don't know . . . I was a totally different person. She put her hand on my thing!"

"What Charlie!" I said without even thinking.

"She put her hand on my thing and I was surprised as to how good it felt. No. How good it felt. Really good!"

Suddenly, I was beyond being shocked and as he told me the rest of his story, I remember thinking, 'Charlie is sick.' He has lost his mind. He has lost his identity, for sure, as he had said! Forget his dim-witted questions he used before to come onto women in a club. Was this a dumb or fantastic act? "Dumber" than anything I have ever heard . . . Stupid and dumb. Aah! . . . The perils of alcohol. Father was right about alcohol all along.

"Well! Before we could do anything we would later regret, Sophie stormed into my bedroom. She was angry. No, she was as mad as hell. She was screaming her lungs out, "Charlie are you out of your mind?" Startled, I stopped. Aboud stopped.

"The warm softness of Aboud's lips, which had encapsulated me slipped off mine, ending our osculation abruptly, just like a child withdraws her hand caught in a cookie jar," Charlie said.

"Aboud quickly pushed my zipper up and walked out of my bedroom hastily. While I, still laying on my bed, face-up, remained motionless," Charlie added.

"What I said to Sophie next was dumb and stupid. Why did you invite her here and you know I have a high libido?"

"Puzzled, she just stood there, stock-still, looking at me with red-hot eyes dancing in their eye sockets like cherries in a slot machine. Without saying a word, she stormed out of my room as quickly as she had come. I didn't move. I heard her say to her friend, 'Let us go!' I didn't move a muscle. Shortly afterwards, I heard my door fly open and then slam shut, followed by hastened footsteps down our squeaky stairs as the three women descended them. I closed my eyes, wondering what it was that I had done to incense her so much. My ears were attuned to the sound of their footsteps as they made their way down the stairs until they died at the landing. . . I mean, until I could no longer hear them. I must have fallen asleep after that. When I awoke, it was morning and my door was unlocked."

Charlie took a deep sigh, a sigh of relief, having unburdened himself to me. Stupefied, I remained silent for a very long time. There was nothing to say.

"My Sister! . . . I lost my identity last night!" I looked on.

"There you have it! God's honest *truth*. The whole truth, and nothing but the truth. I lost my mind. I lost my identity last night. I lost everything myself last night!" That was all that was left to say.

Sensing my discomfort, Charlie bade me goodbye and hurriedly walked out of my door, his nerves twitching nervously, "Later Mary!" he said, heading for my door. He didn't turn back to look at me. I didn't tell him not to leave.

I listened to Charlie's footsteps as he walked up the stairs until they died to jiggling of his keys as he fumbled with his door. I heard a squeaking sound of his door as it flew open and then fell back behind him. I stood up, walked to my door, pushed its latch in place, and then retraced tracks back to my sofa. I dropped my body onto my couch. It emitted a puff-like sound as I sank into its softness. I remained there for quite a very long time, staring dispassionately at our half drank cups of tea. After Charlie left, I was convinced I had no further intention of writing a letter to Oprah!

Though, I began to think: 'Hadn't we all lost our identity? Somehow? The moment we set foot in a classroom door back home, didn't we lose our identity? By virtue of being Christianized, didn't we lose our identity? How about our names? I wondered if Charlie had not changed his name from something like Obi Okparocha to Charlie Crabtree. Didn't he lose his identity that way? Take me, for example, when I changed my name to Mary? Wasn't I shading off a part of my Logooli identity? The moment we set foot into the womb of the two-winged bird that glides in the clouds, didn't we lose our identity? By virtue of setting foot onto American soil, didn't we lose our identity? That night, I went to bed on an empty stomach.

19

I awoke Saturday morning at the twilight of dawn to a loud deafening sound of my quartz alarm clock. Irked by its disruption of my sleep, I slammed my hand on the snooze button. It felt cold to the touch. I quickly tucked my hand under the blanket determined to sleep a little longer. I drifted back to sleep only to be startled to my pulsing present by an all too familiar clop-like footsteps of someone ascending up the stairs. Without doubt, I knew it was Sam and the day of my reckoning had finally dawned. Without thinking, I jumped out of bed, and sprinted towards my living room to find my purse. I was delighted because I had been paid the previous day and cashed the check. My rent was safely zipped in the synthetic perforated side of my purse. I fumbled around looking for my purse, but I couldn't find it. As the footsteps drew closer to my door, I raced back into my bedroom. I went straight to my dresser, even though I knew I rarely put my purse there. There was nothing on top. I pulled the top drawer. Still, there was no purse save for a pile of my ragged looking underwear. They were all faded in color and fit for a dumpster. I pushed the drawer back in place. I slid my closet door open. Similarly, there was nothing. So, I just stood there puzzled, unable to locate my damn purse. I felt as though the purse had grown wings. I heard a fist banging hard on my door. I counted each distinctive knock—One. Two. Three. Four. The fifth one was followed by a soft jiggling of my door knob. Another systematic bang followed! Bang! Bang! The knob jiggled again causing my heart to race. Right then, I knew Sam was going to enter my apartment any second, whether I liked it or not. I must have latched the door because if I had not, he would have already entered my living room with his alcohol dulled eyes. I could still hear him fervently struggling with the knob while I pulled open everything I had in my apartment worthy of opening. He joggled the door several more times. Unable to force it open, I heard him fumble with his keys, followed by a sound of their jiggling. I wasn't surprised when I heard him push a key in my door knob, turned it as its latch flew open at an instant click.

Sam was inside my apartment now. Phew! What a disaster. I hadn't found my purse. I ran back to my living room puppy-eyed, hoping to beg him for mercy again. I knew he wouldn't believe me. Even the idea that his action might have been illegal never crossed my mind.

No sooner had I walked into the living room, than I saw Sam's red-hot eyes. I couldn't ask him now; he wouldn't listen to my excuse even if it was the honest truth, a truth which was irrefutably irrelevant to him. I imagined him thinking, 'What dimwit misplaces a purse anyway?'

"Mary," I heard Sam call my name in a gruff voice. "Why didn't you open the door when I knocked?" I didn't answer him.

"I have come to collect my rent! And for the heavens of me, no more excuses please."

"Mr. Snackwell," I said timidly, addressing him with the title "Mr.," even if I knew he probably didn't deserve it. "I am sorry, but I have misplaced my purse. Inside, was your rent money!" No sooner had I uttered those fateful words, than Sam's jaws fell open, as a macabre smile began to form at the corner of his mouth. You know the kind of smile intended as scorn. All was quiet. Out of fear, I stepped back, further and further away from Sam lest he seek to bury his nails into my tender flesh like he had done before.

"You d—n b—h, I want my money this very minute!"

"Mr. Snackwell, I just can't find my purse," I insisted. If only you could give me a few minutes, I could try to locate it."

"Ha ha ha ha," he laughed ominously, a laughter which sent a cold shiver down my spine. "Your African ass is mine now!"

"No, you don't. I have your rent, *Mr.* Snackwell!" I said, emphasizing the word Mr. "If only I could find my purse!"

He couldn't and didn't hear a word I said. Instead, Sam flew into a rage. "I want my money right now. Drop it right here," he said opening the palm of his right hand.

Defeated, my body broke into a cold sweat. I wanted to run away from him to my bedroom. I wanted to protect my little belongings convinced he would surely evict me, throw me and all my earthly possessions to the streets. But I couldn't run. My feet felt heavy as though weighted with lead. Sensing my discomfort, Sam continued to threaten me, thrusting his fist hard on my coffee table again and again and again.

Frightened, my body broke into a cold sweat until I was drenched. I moved towards my couch, sat down, and rested my head between my knees and put my hands to my ears blocking the sound of Sam's voice. I emerged from my dream to the distant sound of my alarm clock resonating louder than Sam's fist crushing hard against my coffee table.

Forcing my eyes open, I glanced at the neon light of my quartz alarm clock. The time read 5:30 a.m. and my eyes were still heavy with sleep. I felt like crawling back to sleep and hide behind my covers forever. Unfortunately, I couldn't. I had approximately forty-five minutes to get ready for work that morning. It was supposed to be my day off, but I had taken on extra hours to offset Sam's imposed late fee on my rent. It was only a half day shift. Nothing to fret about.

6:30 a.m. Having quenched my caffeine addiction on Folgers's Fresh Roast coffee, I felt ready to face the world. I walk into the womb of the universe smiling gleefully with unabashed eyes. I was ready to combat all my demons, Sam Snackwell and the nauseating smells of St. Grace.

Elated, I grabbed my purse, keys in hand, taking my first stride into the world. Stepping outside my doorsteps, my eyes vacantly stared to the east where daylight begins, mesmerized by the sun's bright fingers spread across the eastern hemisphere. A cool mist brushed softly against my face. Filled with the awe and wonder of earth's majestic nature, I froze, inhaling in the fresh scents of the morning. I opened and closed my eyes again and again feeling the cool wind continue to brush against my bare skin. Before I could muster courage to walk down the stairs, I glimpsed at Charlie's apartment wondering if he was awake or if he had gone to work. Right then, an image of a disheveled Charlie I had seen the previous night returned to me. His squeamishness after divulging his taboo secrets began to gnaw me—why did he choose to tell me all about it? I cursed myself for not telling him, 'I understand you completely!' It happens to the best of us. Maybe, I should have told him, 'It was definitely the drink!' even if I wasn't certain of it. I didn't. Instead, I was shaken to the core by his *truth* to muster the courage of true friendship, not consumed by his divulged his dark secret. "Damn Charlie!" I mumbled as these words simply slipped softly off my lips.

Another cool draft passed brushing against my exposed skin. I could feel it to my bare bones, a coolness which reeled me back to my pulsing present. I had to make haste to work or risk facing Joyce's wrath. As I descended the stairs, I barely heard its creaking for I had become desensitized to it. Instead, I heard the howling whistle of the wind blowing hard against the rooftops of Crystal Lake Apartments. Step one. Step two. Step three, I steadily descended the stairs. The cool wind made my eyes water. Tiny beads of tears formed at the corner of my eyes and glided downward staining my cheeks. Without bothering to dry them, I hastened my steps downwards—four. Five. Six. At the base of the stairs, I hastened my pace to my white Honda Civic, *my* diamond. As always, I struggled to open her door, an act to which I had become accustomed . . . "Next year, I must buy a new car," I mumbled. "Not really brand new, but a brand new used car." I stepped into the driver's seat, started the car and revved the engine. It purred like a kitten's gentle purr. Elated, I knew I would have a good day.

As expected, my day was uneventful. Nothing to speak of happened. Before going back home, I went straight to Kroger and bought my some ingredients for supper. I had made a solemn promise to treat myself to a taste of home. I had, all week long, craved *Ugali*, chicken, and *sukuma wiki*. Aah! Sheer goodness. There was nothing better than homemade food! And as I had willed, so it was . . . A fantastic Kenyan supper!

20

Dinner alone, of *ugali*, chicken, and *sukuma wiki*, was fabulous. Nothing in this world could have surpassed it. It was simply divine. I cut little amounts of *ugali* with my fingers, formed a small round ball in my palm, and created a tiny hole in the ball with my thumb. Kids back home called it 'remote control.' I used it to scoop the soup and then dropped the ball into my mouth. I felt the juices burst in my mouth as I gently crushed the food between my teeth. Uuh! Uuh! Marvelous. I took small bites of the chicken, followed with *sukuma wiki*. Time and again, I formed ball after ball and scooped the soup. I ate and ate and ate, until I could swallow no more morsel. Just then, I felt a sense of peacefulness encompass me—a relief from my week-long stressful days.

I reclined on my couch as I routinely did. I curled my body, yet again, on it, wrapped it in my comforter and closed my mind and eyes to everything, and the world. For a while, I forgot all about Charlie. I forgot all about Sam Snackwell and his threats of my eviction. I forgot all about Bill. I forgot all about Mama Joy and Grandma Tufroza. I was at peace with myself. It was a feeling I had not experienced in a very long time.

Before long . . . about 5:00 p.m. I heard soft thudding sounds of rain against my window. So soft they were—ta ta ta tata—they inspired in me a desire to watch a good romantic comedy to dazzle my mind. I thought of movies like *When Harry Met Sally*; *An Almost Perfect Affair*; *Forces of Nature*; *Runaway Bride*, or *Sleepless in Seattle*. I had none; instead, I settled for the evening news. I liked being current on what was going on in the world. I turned on the T.V.

and flipped through the channels settling for CBS News. There were latest reports on the war in Iraq. The on-going conflict between the Israelis and the Palestinians. Afghanistan. Al Qaeda. The presidential campaigns of 2004. The latest commercials in which John Kerry was bashing Bush. Or George W. Bush's commercials in which he was bashing Kerry. Unfortunately, instead of news briefs on the aforementioned, images of American civilians killed in Falluja, Iraq, with their bodies dragged in the streets, burnt, and mutilated filled the tube. While others, their bodies were hanged on a bridge like meat in butchery.

Suddenly, the peacefulness which had enveloped me a moment ago vanished. Instead rage, unsurpassed rage, ambushed me. I couldn't understand man's inhumanity to man. I thought of a mother's pain for the loss of her child. What a pain a father must feel for the loss of his child. I abhorred war with all its horrors. My heart ached for those mothers and fathers, husbands and wives, brothers and sisters, son and daughters who would soon be recipients of unidentifiable remains of their loved ones. As the chilling video clip of the dead Americans came to an end, I turned my television off feeling helpless, my mind in utter disarray. With my body still curled-up on my couch, I closed my eyes once more to the world, not wanting to bear witness to its violence, something with which I struggle to this day. Outside, the rains of despair continued to fall in slow and steady flow, tapping and tapping at my window. I tried to sleep off the images I had just seen, but I couldn't. Just then, I recalled a poem I had written several years ago on carnage in Rwanda, a genocide which was sparked by the death of President Juvenal Habyarimana whose plane was shot down above Kigali airport on 6 April 1994 on his way from talks in

Tanzania. It came from the heart and lacked poetic form. But there it was filled with vivid images of decapitated bodies of the innocent sacrificed in the name of freedom. They were as vivid today as they were then.

Boom! Boom!
Sounds of gunfire
disrupt a mother's sleep
as her children are massacred
by those whom she calls kindred,
a melancholy song of Africa's modern day atrocities.

Blatantly sadistic,
the sight of dead bodies scattered
over the sunny-baked African landscape
agonize bereaved relatives whose future
linger on the brink of desperation
their looming death epitomized
by the mutilated bodies of their children,
a true hymn of Africa's backlog of imperialism.

Blatantly sadistic,
horrid corpses of a mother, father, wife, husband,
son, daughter, brother, sister grandmother and grandfather
mark an end to the brotherhood and sisterhood of man.

Boom! Boom!
Sounds of gunfire rave the air, ravaging villages
and one by one, men and women like ants,
drop at the hands of their enemies

their mutilated bodies dragged in dust and heap-like piled
like Mt. Kiliminjaro over the green landscape of Africa
while revolutionists on a freedom call
seek to cleanse Rwanda of its impurities.

Trillions of flies hover and feast
on decomposed bodies of the dead denied proper burial
as though the land upon which they lie were a house of slaughter
mothers whose children are stripped off in death
wail over the carnage in their midst
as the stench of decomposed bodies
engulf the air beyond the borders of Rwanda,
while the living in a single file steal thief-like to Tanzania's borders.

Yet, remember,
Tutsis, in Rwanda, fallen victim to their brother's sword
could be you or me
could be Kabarondo, Rukumbeli, Kibungo,
Mukarange, Iraqs, Afghanistans, Kenyans, Ugandans, or Somalians
turn not a deaf ear to the sounds of gunfire in Rwanda
turn not a deaf ear to the sounds of gunfire in Somalia
turn not a deaf ear to the suffering of Africa's children
for Africa's children are my children, your children, our children.

The blood of the dead Tutsis
baptizes the land reminding us
of the price Africa pays as her children untimely die
leaving scars too deep to heal!

These thoughts of a chaotic world triggered by images of dead Americans in Iraq flashed on my mind and ended as fast as they had begun. I replaced the images of the dead Tutsis with those of dead Iraqis; only this time, instead of having the booming sounds of gunfire, I saw rolling tankers against the sandy Iraq landscape and the hovering ruckus of the stealth bombers above the nightly Baghdad skies. Sighing deeply, I closed my mind just as I had closed my eyes for there was nothing more to be said or done, but despair.

This way, my evening came and went. Sam Snackwell didn't show-up at my doorsteps that evening. Neither did I hear from my friend Charlie . . . He didn't call me and I didn't call him. "I should have said something to him last night," I thought. Acknowledged, at the very least, to him that he might have had a temporary lapse of memory and yielded to temptations. I wondered if someone must have slipped a *mickey* in his drink, naming *it a* culprit for his misjudgment as he claimed.

When I went to bed that night, I dreamt of a "weeping" moon. Its yellow shafts of light seeped into my bedroom through the gaping blinds of my window. Its sighting caused my body to shudder. And next to my bed, stood Mama Joy. Her eyes were bloody red and she was waggling her index finger annoyingly in my direction. She spoke to me in an icy voice, "Beware of the weeping moon my child! A weeping moon is always evil and sinister . . . A harbinger of wickedness concealed from those destined for its punishment." I wanted to ask her what all this meant, but I couldn't talk—my lips moved, but no words fell off them. Mama's warning reminded me of the howling cry of an owl, a bird of ill omen. My people believed its hooting was a prelude to a death. I also thought of other things she might have told me about it. "My child . . . if you see a weeping moon, be vigilant. Avoid arm's length of danger. Guard yourself, will you?' But Mama Joy had not just warned me against the perils of a weeping moon. She had also warned me against other things too. She had warned me about men. She had warned me against sex. She had warned me against alcohol like father had. She had warned me against cigarettes. I awoke from my dream a rattled girl. So, I laid in my bed, recalling Mama's words, and wondering what the 'weeping' moon meant in my life. Soon, I realized the weeping moon, whose yellow shafts of light continued to slip into my room through my gaping blinds, was no dream. It was my reality, a looming reminder of lurking danger to my being. This truth sent a shiver down my spine. I shook my body vigorously and then drifted back to slumber, not thinking of those still awake—night-runners, thieves, and insomniacs.

21

I opened my eyes to a stormy and thunderous Sunday morning. It was as though the heavenly bowels had finally opened up upon us. Having no plans that morning, I pulled the covers above my head determined to sleep until noon, or until the rains subsided.

I had no such luck. I had not even drifted back to sleep when I heard sounds of heavy footsteps of someone running up our stairs. Immediately, my stomach churned for no apparent reason. I wondered if it was Charlie returning home. He was always a night owl. I also knew the person running up the stairs couldn't have been Sam coming to collect rent. It was too early for him to do so. He wasn't an early riser. He usually came between 4:00 p.m. and 5:00 p.m. when he was certain his tenants were home. The time on my clock read 8:05 a.m.

When I heard the loud banging sound on my door! Bam! Bam! Bam! I froze. My door rattled nearly breaking. I couldn't go back to sleep now. Pushing my covers off, I left the comfort of my bed, grabbed my house robe, knotting its belt around waist as I straddled towards the living room. Bam! Bam! Bam! The sound continued and the door rattled again. Right away, I knew it wasn't Charlie either.

No sooner had I pulled open my door, than I saw it wasn't Charlie after all, but Sam Snackwell. His breath wasn't tainted with the smell of alcohol as always. Perhaps, he must have spent his entire week at Mary Haven detoxification center off of Alum Creek Road. That had to be it. It was the only rational explanation as to why he hadn't come to collect my rent earlier in the week as he had threatened.

"Good morning Miss Mary," he said. I was startled by his show of politeness. Sam never wasted time on politeness.

"Good morning to you too Mr. Snackwell," I said.

He stood there, looking at me like a stooge for a fraction of a second, sizing me up. I didn't give him chance to ask me for his rent money. Instead, I said, "Wait here a second!" He did. He didn't invade my space this time, but stood right outside my entrance door and awaited my return.

I walked back a few steps into my living room, all the way to my coffee table where I had laid an envelope on which I had inscribed his name. Enclosed inside was my rent in full. Next to it, was my T.V. guide. I picked up the envelope, walked back to the door, and handed it to Sam.

"Thank you Miss," he said.

"You are most welcomed," I said. He turned his back to me, facing Charlie's apartment. I walked away from him ready to close my door. On second thought, I stopped and looked in his direction. "Mr. Snackwell," I said. He turned his head to look at me. "Thank you for giving me an extension on my rent." With a grin-like smile and a slight wave of his hand, he made a gesture, which indicated to me it was no problem at all. I closed the door behind me, walked back to my bedroom, turned off my telephone ringer, and went back to sleep.

When I woke up later that day, it was shortly after noon and the rains had long subsided. Shafts of light cast a glow into my bedroom. Feeling hungry, I remembered my *ugali* and *sukuma* from the previous night. I ate it for a late lunch and it tasted much better than the previous night.

22

Later that afternoon, as I sat watching *Trading Places,* an American comedy directed by John Landis, I heard a ruckus outside my door. The words which were being uttered, bellowing above the sound of my television, were so vulgar I dare not repeat them here. I muted my television to listen. The noise was coming from the direction of Charlie's apartment and became increasingly louder without the T.V. on. Without thinking, I stood up and stormed-out of my door into the womb of the universe like a mad woman held captive by a hypnotic disturbance. Though I was open-eyed, I wasn't sure of what I was about to see. No sooner had I set foot outside than I saw Charlie. His hands were in a firm entanglement and held captive by a man whom I would later learn to be Sam Snackwell's hired hand, and Charlie's evictor. Immediately, an odd feeling, a sense of foreboding filled me. The two men were bull-locked in a fist fight. With them, were two other men raggedly dressed in blue overalls fitting for the task at hand; one was short and chubby; while the other was tall and skinny. The two men were indifferent to Charlie just like their accomplice who was working hard to restrain Charlie from halting their mission—the eviction. The two were engrossed in their undertaking, like worker ants, as though divorced from the brawl. They rushed in and out of Charlie's house, passed the fighting men, and emerged hauling his belongings, from his frayed sofa, tattered in its corners, a coffee table, end tables, and anything and everything they could get their hands on, once of value to him, but now had the façade of worthless.

Hurriedly, the men lugged Charlie's personal belongings and scattered them outside his door onto the asphalt pavement of our parking lot. They tossed all of it outside like garbage. Stumped, I stopped right in front of my door, not daring to move an inch while I rubbed my fingers against my temples. And like a flash, my mind took flight to a dream I had had the previous night. Everything was clear and real now as it was in my dream. I remembered thinking of how Sam would come to evict me, and scattered my belongings onto the pavement of our parking lot if I hadn't had my rent paid. I thought of how anger could have crept into my veins, unable to convince him of having misplaced my purse. And he, pig-headed, wouldn't have heard a word of what I said. He would have stared at me contemptuously. My knees would have jelled as I sagged low at my ankles nearly falling. Feelings of sadness and embarrassment would have enveloped me all at once. In my dream, I was stupefied with my eviction, just as much as I was by Charlie's forceful eviction. Afraid to fall from the agony of witnessing a friend cast out of his house like a dog, I leaned onto the guard-rail.

"Goddamn it! Get the f—k out of my sight!" Charlie raved. "You cannot do this to me. . . You son of b—h!" But the man, distraught, merely said, "I am simply doing my job man . . . Just doing my job."

After that, the man paid Charlie no attention. Though that didn't stop Charlie from his obscene rant of "Goddamn it . . . F—k you! Gee Wheez! What am I supposed to do now?" The more Charlie raved, the more his evictor restrained him, firmly pushing him out of his door to make it easy for his companions to have easy access to the apartment. While Charlie's feet were securely grounded at his entrance door, supported by its ledge, his hands and those of his assailant were still knotted and, both men, gave the impression of two bulls tightly locked in a tag of war with neither man willing to give up. I wondered if calling the police would be in order under such circumstances, but I couldn't because I knew that would put Charlie in more trouble. His evictors had the eviction papers to back them. Charlie had nothing, but the tail between his legs. I dismissed the whole idea of calling the police as my mind took flight again to my dream. I could now see Sam's menacing brown eyes gawking at me; his voice bellowing into my ears, "You African d—n b—h! Drop my rent money here!" His palm was spread wide, but I couldn't find my purse. His attitude made me experience a self-loathing feeling as though my mere presence in his midst was as insignificant as a fly prostrating on a heap of dung. My face was sullen with grief, powerless and shy like a mimosa plant at the touch of a finger. I curled on my couch, praying for Sam to leave me alone, but he couldn't until he had completely put me in my rightful place . . . a dark place searing with nothing more than loneliness and emptiness. To Sam, I was insignificant! Charlie, too, was insignificant to his assailants, for they had a job to do and doing it they were!

I was reeled back to my pulsing present with the sound of loud glass shattering, one of Charlie's blue lamps cast outside onto the pavement. "Oooh!" I gasped in fright as I saw small blue shards of glass scattered everywhere. I promised myself to avoid stepping on them when I walked around the parking lot later on in the day. I felt a choking lump crop in my throat as tears began to sting the rims of my eye-lids as though I was the ill-fated daughter of woman cast into the cold open. While Charlie, on the other hand, struggled much harder now with his evictor as though he had acquired some mysterious strength. Soon, I heard police sirens piercing the air. Someone, a neighbor, must have seen the unfolding drama and called the police. "Oh brother! Charlie is in trouble now," I said softly.

Sensing trouble, Charlie loosened his grip around the man's hands. Free at last, the man shoved him forward, as he stepped into Charlie's apartment with a swagger. I watched him until he vanished behind the door and until it had fallen back into place with a bang. Straddling forward, Charlie nearly fell off the stairs, but he grabbed the railing, finally finding firm ground. Dazed, he walked down one more step, and then plopped his bottom on the former. His posture reflected an image of a man whose virility had been thwarted. Eyes to the ground, he remained mute. At the same time, the policemen, who had just arrived to the scene much too late to intervene, killed the siren and the engine of their car, but the flashing red and blue lights remained on. I watched Charlie as though the arrival of the men of the law had no bearing to his life. I felt for him because I, too, had narrowly escaped an eviction. I, too, would have been cast out into the streets like a dog had Joyce, my boss, not given me a loan of a hundred dollars to off-set the balance I needed to have my rent paid in full. Charlie made no effort to acknowledge the policeman.

"What seems to be the problem here," I heard the policeman say as he strode towards our apartment, and stopped at the staircase landing. His hands were to his gun the entire time.

"Nothing at all," Charlie lied, though I knew he knew the truth already, whatever that *truth* was.

"Someone called about a disturbance!" he said sharply, his eyes pinned on Charlie and inspecting him, from head to toe. My eyes glossed over him in a twinkling. Slowly, I turned my head sideways to steal a glance at Charlie. I shrugged my shoulders, but Charlie dared not lift his head. The man with whom he was fighting emerged from the house lugging Charlie's coffee table, which he tossed to the already growing pile of stuff. Charlie gritted his teeth. Seeing the policeman, as though he wasn't aware of his presence, the man descended the stairs to explain to him what had just transpired.

I watched the two men walk several yards away from the stairs' landing, way beyond earshot. I couldn't hear their conversation, but I didn't need to. I knew what they were discussing, Charlie's stubbornness to allow a smooth eviction. I couldn't blame him. A warm apartment was worth fighting for. Had I been the one facing the evictors' clutches, I would probably have fought for my safe haven crazed out of my mind, even more than Charlie.

A minute later both men began walking back towards us. As they drew closer to the stairs, the policeman stopped a few feet away from the landing, not daring to set foot on those creaky steps, but Charlie's evictor ascended them. I couldn't move my eyes away from the police, afraid to even blink my eyes lest I miss seeing something important. The policeman, with a strong show of arrogance, his right hand clasping hard on his gun securely fastened onto his belt on his right side, admonished Charlie. "No more trouble mister! You hear . . . or else, I am going to throw you in jail!" He released his grip around his gun, patted it gently, letting Charlie know he was the boss. He meant every word of it. Charlie, whose face was sullen and with his eyes to the ground, didn't utter a word. He simply nodded his head in agreement. He knew the police had power over him and he couldn't argue with that kind of power. Unlike Charlie, I stared at the policeman dispassionately. Charlie's prized possessions were now strewn on the pavement like junk waiting to be hauled to a dumpster.

When Charlie's eviction was over and the three men and the policeman were long gone, the sun was almost concealed behind the clouds in the western hemisphere. The horizon hemorrhaged as the sky darkened into a bruised blue. Charlie still sat on the steps, his head downcast, and his face sagged as he looked at his belongings scattered on the black asphalt like a formidable decoration. He looked like a fossil in a museum. He didn't twitch a muscle from when he had plopped his bottom on the steps at the policeman's arrival. I, too, had not moved. I had been transformed into a poster board at my doorstep.

Slowly, I gathered courage and I walked to Charlie. Gently, I put my hand on his shoulder determined to tell him, "My brother, I am sorry for your troubles," but I couldn't. Sorry was not enough. Instead, I invited him into my apartment, a part of me wanting to offer him a cup of my best Kenyan tea, which would help him calm his nerves. Not daring to look into my eyes lest I judge him, he shushed me. Though, honestly speaking, I couldn't have judged him. Who knows, next month I could be him. I felt his pain . . . A pain which lacerated my heart with a lot of hurt. Certainly, Charlie didn't know that I, too, came close to being evicted, a truth until now had been my secret. I begged him to come into my apartment twice, but he adamantly refused. Defeated, I walked away from him, pulled my door open as it emitted a loud creaking sound. I slammed it behind me as I heard its latch fall into place with an annoying click. I didn't lock it this time.

Once inside, I found my way straight to my refrigerator. Without thinking, I pulled the door open, reached out for a gallon of milk and poured myself a brim-filled glass to calm my nerves. I was too tired to make a cup of hot tea, but delighted Charlie had turned down my offer. With each sip I took, my past enfolded into my present. As I guzzled the last drop of my milk, it left a crescent moon on my dark upper lip, which I dared not wipe. Then, I put my glass on the table and curled my body on my couch, curved it like Grandma Tufroza's back. I laid there motionless, my present fusing into my past and back to present. Visions of me soaring up in the sky, propelled in a two metallic winged bird as it sliced through thick white fluffy clouds to the sunny baked landscape of Kerongo, became my reality. I was tranquil again. At home with family. One-by-one I saw them showering me with smiles, melting my heart with delight. I was there with them—safe and sound. Safe with my brothers and sisters. Safe with Mama. Safe with Father. There would be no more Charlie Crabtree or Sam Snackwell to haunt my waking days. There would be no loneliness. These visions were merely conduit to my fragmented life. I closed my eyes as the sun sank below the western horizon leaving behind massive strokes of red on the hazy Ohio sky. As darkness fell, I knew I wasn't the only restless soul under the God's remote tent of sky.

Mmap Fiction Series

If you have enjoyed **Fragmented Lives** consider these other fine books in **Mmap Fiction and Drama Series** from *Mwanaka Media and Publishing:*

The Water Cycle by Andrew Nyongesa
A Conversation..., A Contact by Tendai Rinos Mwanaka
A Dark Energy by Tendai Rinos Mwanaka
Keys in the River: New and Collected Stories by Tendai Rinos Mwanaka
How The Twins Grew Up/Makurire Akaita Mapatya by Milutin Djurickovic and Tendai Rinos Mwanaka
White Man Walking byJohn Eppel
The Big Noise and Other Noises by Christopher Kudyahakudadirwe
Tiny Human Protection Agency by Megan Landman
Ashes by Ken Weene and Umar O. Abdul
Notes From A Modern Chimurenga: Collected Struggle Stories by Tendai Rinos Mwanaka
Another Chance by Chinweike Ofodile
Pano Chalo/Frawn of the Great by Stephen Mpashi, translated by Austin Kaluba
Kumafulatsi by Wonder Guchu
The Policeman Also Dies and Other Plays by Solomon A. Awuzie

Soon to be released

Sword of Vengeance by Olatubosun David

https://facebook.com/MwanakaMediaAndPublishing/

Printed in the United States
by Baker & Taylor Publisher Services